Richmond upon Thames Libraries

Renew online at www.richmond.gov.uk/libraries

LONDON BOROUGH OF
RICHMOND UPON THAMES

I've always adored *The Hobbit* by J. R. R. Tolkien – so when I discovered that he had been inspired by an older fantasy story, *The Marvellous Land of Snergs* by E. A. Wyke-Smith, I had to find it! I loved the story but it was a bit old-fashioned in places – so the marvellous Veronica Cossanteli has now reimagined it for today's young readers. The result is wise, funny, charming and full of adventure – there are cinnamon bears, magical forests, a motley sailing crew and of course the Snergs themselves, little human-like creatures with tons of courage (and quite a bit of foolishness!). I think you'll love it, just like Tolkien and *his* children did.

BARRY CUNNINGHAM
Publisher
Chicken House

THE MARVELLOUS LAND OF SNERGS

VERONICA COSSANTELI

Based on the original by E. A. Wyke-Smith

Illustrated by Melissa Castrillón

Chicken House

2 Palmer Street, Frome, Somerset BA11 1DS
www.chickenhousebooks.com

Text © Veron

From a concept by Chic
based on E. A. Wyke-Smit
originally published in Grea
To his memory and with th

Illustrations © Melissa Castrillón 2020

First published in Great Britain in 2020
Chicken House
2 Palmer Street
Frome, Somerset BA11 1DS
United Kingdom
www.chickenhousebooks.com

Cover and interior design by Helen Crawford-White
Cover and interior illustrations by Melissa Castrillón
Typeset by Dorchester Typesetting Group Ltd
Printed and bound in Great Britain by CPI Group (UK) Ltd, Croydon CR0 4YY

The paper used in this Chicken House book is made from wood grown in sustainable forests.

1 3 5 7 9 10 8 6 4 2

British Library Cataloguing in Publication data available.

PB ISBN 978-1-911490-60-9
eISBN 978-1-913322-66-3

For Xander, with thanks for so much laughter along the way
and for all those walks.

To everyone who knew and loved this book as it was, a word of apology.
I have done my best to keep to the spirit of the original but stories are
living things and this one proved more boisterous than most.
Let loose from its covers, it behaved much like Tiger the puppy,
hurtling off without warning in unexpected directions.
All I could do was follow. Forgive me.

Also by Veronica Cossanteli

The Extincts
The Halloweeds

In which rules are broken
and Miss Watkyns is displeased.
Captain Vanderdecken's Band
Practice is disturbed, a stranger
arrives in Sunny Bay and
two children, plus a puppy,
pass through a gate and find
themselves Somewhere Else.

CHAPTER 1

'Children need rules,' stated Miss Watkyns. 'And rules must be obeyed.'

A lady made of angles and straight lines, neat and crisp all the way from her hairpins to the hem of her long black skirts, Miss Watkyns believed in good manners, fair play, plenty of fresh air for growing children – and rules.

She sat, straight and stiff, at a large desk where nothing was ever allowed to be out of place. Even the goldfish in its crystal bowl swam in orderly clockwise circles. Behind her, the open window let in sea-salty sunshine, the whoops and cries of children let loose to play and the mew of gulls.

Before her were the three rule-breakers: a girl, a boy and a small person who was not a child and should have known better.

Flora sat silent and still, half-hidden behind her cloud of fair hair. There was a faraway-ness about Flora, the look of someone who kept her thoughts and feelings to herself. Next to her, the thin boy with grazed knees was fidgeting, legs swinging, dark eyes bright and watchful. Pip had grown up wary: at the first sign of trouble, he was ready to duck and bolt.

The bench Pip and Flora were sitting on had a name at the Sunny Bay Home for Superfluous and Accidentally Parentless Children. It was known as the telling-off bench, its wood worn smooth by the shuffle of so many guilty behinds. Flora and Pip knew that bench well – but, for now, the telling-off was happening to somebody else.

'The children at Sunny Bay do not *starve*, Mr Gorbo,' Miss Watkyns informed the short, round person standing in front of her. Not much of him reached above the desktop, although he was as grown up as he'd ever be. 'They are fed a carefully balanced diet, with extra custard on Sundays and plenty of prunes. A well-regulated stomach leads to a well-regulated mind. So, can you explain why I find these two,' she glanced at Pip and Flora, 'in a place where they shouldn't be, at a time when they shouldn't be, covered in crumbs and jam?'

Gorbo's sigh was gusty. 'No harm in a few jam tarts, surely? One little midnight feast? "A slice of pie helps the night go by", as my mother used to say.'

'Rules were broken. There is always harm in *that*.' Miss Watkyns was firm. 'The children were caught in the linen cupboard, where they are not allowed, eating between meals, which is not allowed. Accepting food from strangers is not allowed . . .'

'Gorbo's not a stranger,' objected Pip. 'He's our friend.'

'. . . and being out of bed, after Lights Out,' continued Miss Watkyns, ignoring the interruption, 'is *strictly forbidden*. I cannot have children wandering about in the dark. Any number of unpleasant things could befall them, from splinters to untimely death.'

Gorbo hung his head in shame.

'Perhaps Mr Gorbo has not read the rules,' suggested

Miss Scadging, Sunny Bay's matron. A comfortable cushion of a lady with twinkly eyes, she had been an orphan at Sunny Bay herself once upon a time and had never left. She could remember all the way back to the dark days before Miss Watkyns took charge. '*Can* you read, Mr Gorbo?'

'I can't *not* read, exactly.' Gorbo wrinkled his nose at the long list of rules and regulations hanging on Miss Watkyns's wall. 'It depends on what sort of writing and what sort of words, and whether the letters behave as they should. Some of them do squiggle about so. It works better if I do this.' Ducking his head he peered at the rules upside down, from between his legs. 'So, all the cleverness sloshes to my thinking bits . . .'

Pip giggled.

'No sniggering, please.' Miss Watkyns gave him a quelling stare. 'Unkindness is against the rules here at Sunny Bay.'

'I wasn't being unkind.' Pip returned the stare, unquelled. 'Who cares if Gorbo can't read?'

The truth was that Pip couldn't read either. He had begun life in the circus, the smallest member of the Fabulous

Flying Frangipani Family. All he needed to know was how to swing from a trapeze. Nobody had bothered to teach him anything else. When fate brought him to Sunny Bay, he was given a desk in the schoolroom with the other children but education seemed to bounce off him, like raindrops off a duck.

Miss Watkyns turned her attention back to Gorbo.

'Cook is very upset,' she informed him. 'Those jam tarts were for Miss Scadging's birthday tea.'

'I am very fond of strawberry jam,' admitted Miss Scadging.

'I didn't know.' Gorbo unfolded himself, looking very guilty. 'A very happy somethingty-somethingty-some-thingth birthday, Miss Scratching, and a thousand happy returns.'

'Not so many "somethings", if you don't mind,' retorted Miss Scadging. 'I'm forty-three.'

'Hardly more than a child! And here am I, two-hundred and onety-two the last time anybody counted and will I *ever* grow up to behave like a sensible fellow?' Striking his forehead with the flat of his hand, Gorbo sank to his knees.

'O, rascally reprehensible ruffian of a Gorbo!'

'Less of the dramatics, please.' Miss Watkyns was frosty. 'And do stand up, Mr Gorbo. We need to have a little talk. It is several weeks now since you came to Sunny Bay, looking for work. "Any odd jobs", you said – you could turn your hand to anything, you *said*. I have been reviewing your achievements since then.'

'Have you?' asked Gorbo, uneasily.

Putting on her spectacles, Miss Watkyns consulted a list on her desk. 'There was the leak in the attic roof . . .'

'I fixed the hole,' Gorbo assured her. 'Filled it up tight. Not a drop of rain got through . . . until the sun came out and the toffee melted.'

'You told me,' continued Miss Watkyns, 'that you could mend my clock.'

Everybody looked at the mahogany clock on the mantel above the fireplace. It was ticking merrily, but all three of its hands were going backwards.

'Time moves forward, Mr Gorbo,' stated Miss Watkyns. 'That's the way the world works.' She considered her list. 'I don't intend to say much about the shelves you put up in the boys' dormitory – except that it's a pity little Humphrey happened to be underneath when they fell down. It can't be helped; he stopped crying after an hour or two and I daresay the damage isn't permanent.'

'The bleeding has stopped,' confirmed Miss Scadging, 'and the bump is getting smaller.'

Gorbo sagged. 'I clipped your hedges, ma'am,' he offered, in a small voice.

'Yes,' agreed Miss Watkyns, grimly. 'So you did.'

Rising to her feet, she crossed to the window and looked out. Beyond the orphanage walls, the cliff dropped down to the bay where sunlight glittered on the sea and waves licked at the pale, biscuit-crumb sand. There was a fine view across the water to Puffin Island, but Miss Watkyns's gaze rested on her garden. Rowan trees grew to either side of the high iron gates. The children played between low hedges of rosemary and lavender. Here and there, these had been hacked into very peculiar shapes.

'You're quite an artist, Mr Gorbo.'

She didn't mean it, of course, but Gorbo's face brightened. He gave a little skip and went to stand by her side.

'That's my Aunt Flumper, with her best hat on,' he explained, waving a hand at a bush that had been mangled into something like a large toadstool. 'That's a teapot. And *that* one,' he added, with a little bow towards Miss Watkyns, 'was supposed to be *you*. You didn't come out quite right, I'm afraid. It turned into more of a witch . . .'

'A wicked witch?' asked Pip, from the bench.

'Wicked as anything,' agreed Gorbo. 'You can tell by her pointy nose. Like the one out there in—'

'In the stories,' said Miss Watkyns. 'Witches belong in stories. *Only* in stories. I think we all know that.'

Gorbo gave her a doubtful look, fingering the lucky acorn he wore on a string around his neck. 'You might as well say there aren't any goblins or wobsers or squeazels or snotril worms or . . .'

'What's a wobser?' demanded Pip. Even Flora had stirred, behind her hair.

'There's no such thing,' snapped Miss Watkyns. 'Mr Gorbo, kindly refrain from filling the children's heads with the sort of nonsense that will give them nightmares.'

'I'm not scared of any old witch.' Pip was scornful.

Beside him, the sunlight shone on Flora. Sitting so still and quiet, her blue eyes giving nothing away, she looked like a child who had never done or thought anything bad in her whole life.

If I met a witch I'd make her teach me how to turn people into frogs, like in the fairy stories. That, thought Flora, *would serve some people right . . .*

It was three years since Flora had said anything at all out loud. Her thoughts flitted like butterflies, trapped inside her head.

Miss Watkyns had run out of patience. 'I can excuse the roof and the clock and the shelves and poor Humphrey's head,' she told Gorbo. 'And my garden will grow back, in time. But you encouraged these children to break the rules, and that I cannot allow. I'm sorry, Mr Gorbo, but it is time to say goodbye. You are no longer welcome at Sunny Bay.'

There was an unpleasant silence, broken only by the shriek of the gulls and the children playing. Gorbo drooped. Pip frowned. Flora bit her lip. *Not fair.*

'That's not fair.' Pip said it for her. 'Gorbo only took the tarts because we asked him to. He was just being kind.'

'I'm pleased to see that you are ready to take the blame, Pip,' said Miss Watkyns, 'but it doesn't change anything. Mr Gorbo made an unwise decision; now he must face the consequences. I'm sure that he understands that.'

'I should do by now,' sighed Gorbo. 'You sound exactly like my Aunt Flumper.'

Opening a drawer, Miss Watkyns took out a little cloth bag and pushed it across the desk. 'Your wages, Mr Gorbo.'

Gorbo looked surprised. He loosened the drawstring and tipped out the contents. Coins rolled across the desktop. He held one up, to catch the sunlight.

'They're very shiny,' he said politely. 'Who's the beardy fellow?'

Miss Scadging looked shocked. 'That is His Majesty, the King!'

'I'll take just one of him,' Gorbo decided, 'to stick on my wall.' Pulling off his little saucer-shaped cap he bowed first to Miss Scadging and then again, the top of his head almost touching the floor, to Miss Watkyns.

Turning to the children, he dug in his pocket and pulled out some odds and ends of string. 'Goodbye, young half-

Noodles,' he said, handing them each a piece. 'Tie a knot in it, to remember me by. It is how we say goodbye where I come from. May your pie crust always be golden, may your string never fray. Pay attention to Miss Watkyns, for she knows what's what and what's not, and you will grow up sagacious and sensible – not like poor old Gorbo, the very worst of Snergs!'

CHAPTER 2

'What on earth is a Snerg?' Miss Scadging frowned as Gorbo's footsteps faded. 'He was talking very strangely, rambling on about squobsers and weasels.'

'Wobsers,' said Pip. 'And squeazels.'

'*Most* peculiar,' declared Miss Scadging. 'I can't help feeling rather sorry for the little chap. I suppose he has a home to go to – will he manage to find his way?'

'Gorbo knows his way through the woods,' said Miss Watkyns. She frowned into her goldfish bowl. 'I hope he remembers to close the gate . . .'

'The gate?' Miss Scadging was puzzled. 'Which gate?' The

gates at Sunny Bay always stood open. Miss Watkyns trusted her rowan trees to keep out the wrong sort of visitor.

Miss Watkyns pressed her lips together, as if something had slipped through them by mistake, and looked across the desk at Pip and Flora. 'I hope that you two are sorry for the trouble you have caused,' she said, not answering the question. 'To make up for it, you may carry a sack of vegetables to Captain Vanderdecken.'

The Captain's ship, the *Flying Dutchman*, was moored in the next bay. It was a long walk. If they went slowly enough, Pip calculated, they could miss a whole morning in the schoolroom. He would be spared the daily torture of handwriting and arithmetic and geography . . .

'And there's no need to worry about missing lessons,' said Miss Watkyns, who had seen the gleam in his eye. 'Because there won't be any. The other children will be going to Puffin Island, for the picnic.'

There was a moment of shocked silence.

Not the picnic! We can't not go on the picnic!

'Not the picnic!' Pip echoed Flora's silent cry. 'We've been waiting and waiting . . . You never said it was today!'

Picnics at Puffin Island were the best thing about summers at Sunny Bay. They didn't happen often; only when Miss Watkyns decided that they should. She always seemed to arrange it so that the sky was blue, the sea sparkled and the sand was exactly right for building castles. Boats would arrive in the bay to ferry the children to the island. Curious seals would bob their whiskery heads up out of the water, watching with chocolate-drop eyes. Sometimes there were even dolphins. Hampers of sandwiches and pastries and lemonade went with them. There would be swimming and splashing and jumping off rafts, rock pools and leapfrog and Best Sandcastle competitions until at last, with the sun low on the water, they'd sail home – sandy, salty and yawning – for supper and bed.

As Sunny Bay's newest orphans, Pip and Flora had not been to Puffin Island yet but they had heard the other children chattering and knew what they were missing.

Pip was desperate. 'We'll get up extra-early and take the Captain his vegetables tomorrow, before breakfast.'

'He needs them today.' Miss Watkyns was brisk. 'Able Seaman Pollock has mislaid his false teeth and can't chew, so the Crew are having vegetable soup.'

The *Dutchman*'s crew was made up of elderly, retired sailors with very few teeth and no homes of their own. Not a man of them was under seventy; some were nearer ninety. Captain Vanderdecken took them in and kept them sprightly on a strict regime of physical exercise, musket drill and brass band practice.

'The finest crew I ever sailed with,' he often declared. In truth, neither the Captain nor the *Flying Dutchman* had sailed anywhere for a great many years.

Disappointment swelled up and up inside Pip, until it made him lose his temper. 'You're only having the picnic today to be mean, so you can stop us going! Just because of your stupid rules! You make them all up, just to suit you.'

'It is my duty to protect the children in my care and keep them safe,' said Miss Watkyns calmly. 'Without rules, anything can happen. Anything at all.'

'I wish something *would* happen!' stormed Pip. 'I don't care what.' He pointed at the goldfish in its bowl. 'And I bet that fish wishes it too. It has to keep going round and round in that bowl, with nothing else to do, until it gets so bored that it turns upside down and *dies*. You want to keep us like that – but I don't want to be stuck here, being safe!'

Miss Watkyns looked at his flushed face then at Flora, who had disappeared behind her hair again. She experienced a twinge. Was she being too hard on them? *Pull yourself together*, she told herself. *Rules are rules.*

Oh, Miss Watkyns! If only you had paid attention to your twinge! If only Pip and Flora had gone on that picnic, how many dangers and disasters might have been avoided? But whatever's the use of "if only"? Life happens, for better or for worse. Sometimes it all ends happily.

And sometimes it doesn't.

CHAPTER 3

'Keep to the path,' ordered Miss Watkyns. Be polite to the Captain. And absolutely no dawdling.'

It was a gloomy pair that trudged out through the orphanage gates, heaving the sack of vegetables between them. Life had let Pip and Flora down again: they were sorry, but not surprised. Treats and happy times were things that happened to other people. Life was run by grown-ups – and both children had learnt long ago not to expect much of *them*.

Once upon a time, Pip had possessed a mother: a person in spangled tights who did balancing tricks on the back of a white pony. But one moonlit night, Belle the Bareback Bombshell had galloped away from the circus with Stupendous Stefano the Sword Swallower leaving behind her baby son, a sprinkle of sequins and a faint whiff of horse. Left with his father – a wiry, fiery man with fierce fists and a belt that thwacked – things had gone badly for Pip after that. It was a pity, but the smallest and youngest of the Fantastic Flying Frangipanis turned out not to be so fantastic at flying after all. Maybe if his father had been less ferocious, not so quick to shout and thwack, Pip might have done better. He tried his best – tried until he felt sick with nerves and dread – but once you start expecting the worst, it usually happens.

It was the tiger who changed everything, in the end. Wherever the circus stopped, the crowds came to see Boris the Bold and his Bloodthirsty Beast. The Beast was old and threadbare and sometimes, when Pip was in trouble and needed to hide, he would creep between the wheels of her cage. She was less frightening than his father's rages.

Nobody knew how she got out that day. Pip saw her first, from high in the Big Top. The Fantastic Flying Frangipanis were rehearsing their act. The more his father yelled at him, the more Pip got everything wrong. He was dangling from the trapeze – back and forth, to and fro, sicker and sicker – when he saw a striped shape slink between the tent flaps.

'What's the matter with you? What are you waiting for?' His uncles and cousins were stacked in a pyramid, waiting for him to land on top of them. His father was at the very bottom of the pyramid, muscles bulging, face red and shiny with sweat. 'Jump, you spineless little . . .'

His father went on shouting – and the tiger answered; her roar deep and dark and blood-curdling. There was a lot more yelling after that as the pyramid of uncles and cousins came crashing down in a sprawl of twisted limbs. One by one, they picked themselves up – all except for Pip's father . . .

So it was that Pip arrived, superfluous and accidentally parentless, at Sunny Bay – on precisely the same day as Flora.

Flora knew nothing of fierce fathers, or any other kind; hers had been mislaid a long time ago. She had grown up in her own nursery, with a grand dolls' house, a dappled rocking horse and an expensive French governess. Her mother saw her once a day, because she thought she ought to: ten minutes before bedtime was more than enough.

'Motherhood is *exhausting*,' she would complain to her friends. 'I do my best, of course, but she is such an odd little thing and such a chatterbox. She never stops talking . . .'

One spring morning, three years earlier, Flora's governess had taken her for a walk in the park. It was her birthday; after her walk, as a special treat, she was allowed to eat lunch with her mother.

'You should come to the park, Mama, and see the ducks,' Flora had more than usual to say. 'They are very pretty and they quack, you know. Quack, quack. Like that.'

'Don't make silly noises at the table, Flora,' said her mother. She had been at a party the night before, interviewing possible new husbands. She had come home very late and her head was hurting.

'And there was a squirrel,' said Flora. 'It ran up a tree. Wouldn't you like to be able to run up a tree, Mama?'

'Don't speak with your mouth full, Flora,' said her mother.

'And there was a pigeon with only one leg,' pursued Flora.

'Where do you think its other leg went, Mama?'

'Don't shovel your peas up like that, Flora,' said her mother. 'Ladies don't.'

'And,' said Flora, 'there was a man playing the violin. People were putting coins in his hat. I wanted to put one in, but Madame said *non*. Can I go back and see if he is there again tomorrow, Mama?'

'Flora,' said her mother, 'can you never be quiet? You are driving me mad.'

'But Mama, he looked so thin and hungry. I think he needs to buy food. I think . . .'

'Flora, I do not care what you think. I do not care about ducks or squirrels or pigeons or men with violins. STOP TALKING!'

Parents should be careful what they say.

Flora stared at her mother's face, twisted with headache and crossness, and did as she was told. She stopped talking. She didn't say a word – not that day, or the next, or the one after that, or ever since. Even when they came to tell her that the *Titanic* had hit an iceberg and sunk, and that her mother and new father had gone down with it to the bottom of the ocean – Flora hadn't made a sound.

Her other relations were alarmed at the idea of adopting such a strange and silent child. So it was that, superfluous and accidentally parentless, Flora arrived at Sunny Bay – on precisely the same day as Pip.

Standing side by side that first morning, each feeling very much alone as they faced Miss Watkyns in her long black skirts, the two children had drawn closer together – and stayed that way.

'They'll settle in,' said Miss Scadging hopefully, every time they ended up in trouble. 'In time.'

Time passed. Days turned into weeks and weeks into months – and yet Sunny Bay's newest orphans still didn't seem to understand the importance of rules.

The vegetables were heavy in their sack. There wasn't room for Pip and Flora to walk side by side carrying it between them, so they let it sag – dragging it behind them over the rough ground.

'It's all going in a soup, anyway,' reasoned Pip. 'We're actually helping if we squash them a bit.'

Look! Silently, Flora pointed out to sea.

Around the headland came a string of little boats – and down in the bay the orphans of Sunny Bay were walking in two long lines, boys and girls, to meet them. Up on the cliff, Pip and Flora watched with heavy hearts as the boats were tethered and the children piled on board. They could see Miss Watkyns in charge, a tall, angular figure at the end of the jetty. There was Mr Gribblestone with his schoolmaster's gown flapping behind him, and Miss Scadging under her straw hat. They darted here and there like sheepdogs, rounding up the stragglers. The boatmen, in their striped vests, heaved up the picnic hampers then the ropes were untied, and the boats turned their prows towards Puffin Island.

They were growing smaller, well on their way, when the air was split by a deafening BOOM! Seagulls shrieked, scattering skywards.

'Dead Men Doris,' said Pip. 'That means it's twelve o'clock.'

Dead Men Doris was the *Flying Dutchman*'s cannon. She was fired out to sea every day on the dot of noon. Captain Vanderdecken was a stickler for timekeeping.

'Always expect the unexpected,' explained the Captain, who liked to spend a long time each day gazing out to sea through his telescope. 'You never know who's out there!'

With the vegetables bumping behind them, the children tramped on. The gulls had settled after Doris's noonday salute and all was quiet – until they reached the stretch of cliff overhanging the next bay, where the *Flying Dutchman* rocked gently at anchor.

'1 – 2, 3! 1 – 2, 3.' It was Captain Vanderdecken, his voice pitched to carry over the noisiest of storms at sea. '1 – 2, 3! Blow, my hearties, blow!'

The crew were at band practice – playing what may have been the same tune, but not all at the same time. It sounded like a herd of metal cows, bellowing to the beat of a big bass drum.

Flora let go of the sack, putting her hands over her ears. Pip grinned.

Dropping to the ground, he crawled on his stomach to the edge of the cliff and peered over. Down on the beach, the band was on the march. The Captain led the way, beating time with his brass telescope. Behind him, Able Seaman

Pollock staggered under the weight of the drum.

'Put some elbow grease into it!' barked the Captain. 'I can hardly hear you!'

Flora wriggled up to lie beside Pip. They watched as the band, hooting and tooting, reached the far end of the beach where they had to stop to catch their breath.

'Again!' ordered the Captain. 'About turn!'

The cornet went one way; the trombone went another. The euphonium crashed into the flugelhorn.

'Starboard!' roared the captain. 'Tack to starboard!'

Up on the cliff, Pip and Flora stared down into the yawning brass mouth of the tuba. It gaped at the sky, directly beneath them . . . an open goal.

'If only we had a ball . . .' muttered Pip.

Flora was pressing something into his hand: an onion. *Go on – I dare you!*

The onion flew through the air, to land with a terrible clattering *clang* in the jaws of the tuba.

Pip let out a muffled whoop of triumph. 'Beat that!'
Watch me!

Something whizzed past Pip's ear. There was a thunderous

crack as Flora's potato struck the skin of the big bass drum – and went straight through it.

'*Whoa!*' Pip was impressed. 'I didn't know you could throw like that.'

Flora hadn't known it either. Her hand flew up to cover her mouth, but her eyes were laughing.

'We're in for it now,' Pip warned her. 'Look!'

Captain Vanderdecken had his telescope up to his eye, scanning the cliff top. The children squirmed backwards, out of sight. They could never be sure whose leg it was that kicked the sack of vegetables over. Potatoes, onions, cabbages: all began to roll.

The children grabbed at them, but it was no use. Rolling, bouncing, plummeting off the edge – the whole lot rained down on the heads below.

Above the confused cries of 'Enemy fire!', 'Pirates ahoy!' and 'Load the cannon!' rose the wrath of Captain Vanderdecken.

'I know you're up there, young rapscallions! Just you wait until I get my hands on you!'

Pip and Flora didn't wait. They took one look at the chaos

below, joined hands and ran.

If they had obeyed Miss Watkyns's instructions about no dawdling and hurried straight back into the orphanage, their day would have gone very differently. But Pip and Flora had a habit of *not* following instructions, and how were they to know what was just around the corner?

CHAPTER 4

Pip and Flora kept going as far as the orphanage's tall iron gates. There, hot and panting from their race along the cliff, with the Captain's wrath a safe distance behind them, they stopped.

'If we go in,' said Pip, 'we'll only be made to clean out the hen house or peel a million potatoes for Cook. Then the Captain will come and complain about us and we'll be in more trouble.'

It did seem a waste of a fine summer's day . . .

Look. Up there.

Flora was gazing up into the branches of an old pear tree.

It stretched over the orphanage garden wall, dangling green-gold treasure above the children's heads. In less time than it takes to say the words 'climbing trees is absolutely against the rules; it leads to bruises, bumps and broken bones', Pip was up there.

He was lobbing pears for Flora to catch in the skirt of her pinafore when the black car came rattling around the corner.

Motor cars were a rare sight in Sunny Bay. This one had big wheels, a long bonnet and a high roof, and was moving in odd jerks, as if the driver had never been in charge of a steering wheel before.

The children stared as it zigzagged across the road, then shot forwards.

'Flora! Watch out!' yelled Pip.

Flora had already flattened herself against the wall. The car went past them in a rush then stopped dead, in the middle of the road.

'Back!' ordered a woman's voice. 'Make it go backwards!'

There were some clanking, grinding noises, the car rocked this way and that, then came crawling backwards until the rear window was level with the children.

'Stop – *now*,' demanded the voice.

As the car shuddered to a halt Pip swung down from the wall, grazing knees and elbows, to stand beside Flora.

The driver seemed unusually tall, hunched over the steering wheel. His chauffeur's cap was tipped down over his eyes; all the children could see of him was the back of his head, covered in patchy sprouts of hair like the mould on a forgotten potato, and a scrawny, turkey-skin neck. Out of the back-seat window, a lilac-gloved hand was beckoning.

'It must be my lucky day.' The voice was sweet now, sticky-sweet, like candyfloss. Its owner's face was hidden by the wide brim of her elegant lilac hat. A curl of blackberry-dark hair brushed her shoulder; her dress was the purple of ripe plums. 'Dear children, come closer.'

'Why?' asked Pip, not budging. 'What for?'

'For a sugared violet.' The woman held out a flat box containing neat rows of small purple sweets. She popped one into her own mouth. 'They melt on your tongue, you know . . . so delicious.'

Flora, whose long legs made her always hungry, took a step forward. As she had never gone anywhere without her governess before coming to Sunny Bay, nobody had ever thought to tell her about not taking sweets from strangers.

Pip held her back. If he had been born with a trusting soul, life in the circus had knocked it out of him. 'We've got pears,' he said.

'They will give you terrible stomach pains, poor boy,' said the lady, pityingly. 'They are not ripe. Will you not make friends with me? Tell me, is this the Sunny Bay Home for Superfluous and Accidentally Parentless Children? I have come all this way to find a sad, motherless infant whom I may call my own and love and feed on sweeties.'

'They've all gone out,' Pip informed her. 'There's only us. You'll have to come back another day.'

'But,' said the lady, 'you may be exactly what I am looking for! Poor child.' The hat brim tilted towards Flora. 'I cannot bear to think of you locked up in this dreadful place! Are they very unkind to you? I'm sure it must be very grim and miserable, with a great many boring rules. Just imagine, if you came to live with me there would be no rules at all. You could do whatever you liked . . . all day, every day.'

The children hesitated. The lady wore a scent as sweet as

her voice; it drifted up their noses, all the way up into their brains. *No more stupid rules; no more fussing when you broke them . . .*

'I lead a sad and lonely life,' sighed the lady. 'All I ask for is a dear little child to call me Mother. And look what I have here . . .'

On her lap was a small wicker basket. From inside came snuffles, a whine. Unbuckling the straps, the woman held up a puppy – a fuzz of wiry hair, white all over except for something like a black ink blot over one eye and one sooty ear.

A small sound escaped Flora – an indrawn breath. When she was little, before the talking stopped, she had begged for a pet of her own – a dog, a kitten, maybe a white rat; something to which she could tell her secrets. Her mother had shuddered. 'Certainly not,' she had said. 'Think of the hairs and the fleas and the puddles! You already have a nursery full of toys, Flora. What more do you want, you ungrateful child?'

'It could be yours,' said the lady. 'If you want it, you had better come and get it.'

The car door swung open. Scattering pears, Flora started forward. As she reached for the dog, several things happened at once. A yelp from the puppy, a gasp from Flora, a flurry of arms and legs and skirts . . . then the door slammed shut – with Flora on the wrong side.

'Hey!' yelled Pip.

As the car coughed and spluttered into life he threw himself at it, clinging to whatever bit he could.

'Stop – give her back! Let her go!'

It was no use. The woman laughed, poking at him through the window with the sharp point of her purple umbrella until he fell back into the road. The car was still in reverse; he had to roll to escape its wheels. As he picked himself up, it gave a sudden lurch into forward gear and shot off. Pip could see the pale blur of Flora's face at the glass, her mouth open in a silent cry. As the car rounded the corner, a lilac-gloved hand reached out. The puppy dangled, squirming, then dropped into the road.

'Wait!' The soles of his shoes slipping on squelched fruit, Pip set off in pursuit. 'Wait . . . Flora, I'm coming!'

CHAPTER 5

The puppy was still sitting in the middle of the road, looking a little puzzled, his black ear flopped down and his white ear pricked up. He wagged his tail when Pip reached him, before rolling over to have his tummy scratched.

'No time for that.' Pip scooped him up. 'We have to rescue Flora.'

The car might have made a faster getaway with a driver who knew how to drive. As it was it zigged and zagged, bouncing off hedgerows. Even with his arms full of dog, Pip was a strong runner. He kept it in sight until it rounded a bend in the lane and . . . vanished.

Pip came to a breathless halt. Beyond the bend, the road ran on as straight as a ruler – and completely empty.

Cars don't just disappear . . . Pip trotted on, watchful for clues.

There! Wheel tracks. The car had swerved right off the road, crashing through the trees and into the wood.

Wyke Wood was deep and mysterious, as a good wood should be. Sometimes the orphans of Sunny Bay were allowed a little way in – not too far – to gather berries in the autumn, holly boughs and pine cones in winter, bluebells and cowslips in the spring. The children were closely guarded on these expeditions and shepherded home well before dusk. Miss Watkyns always carried a stout stick; she never said why. Now Pip plunged in, following the trail of crushed bracken and bent saplings. *Find Flora.* It was the only thought in his head.

At the sound of voices he ducked behind a hazel bush, holding the puppy close. In the middle of a clearing stood a gnarled old yew. In a wood full of trees, this one was different. Long, long ago lightning had sliced its trunk down the middle. It had healed and grown; now it stood on two legs instead of one. Rammed into one of them was the crumpled bonnet of the car. Seated on a nearby stump with her back to Pip, the lady was straightening her lilac hat. Her large driver stood drooping beside her, blood splashing on to his enormous boots.

'I've known beetroot with more sense than you.' The woman's voice was less like candyfloss now and more like pickled onions. 'Why did I imagine you could do one simple thing without bungling it?'

'Stop, you said,' protested the giant. 'At the Only Yew.'

'Did I tell you to drive straight into it, you lettuce-headed lump? Now look what you've done – we've lost the girl and it is all your fault. Go and look for her!' snapped the lady. 'She can't have gone far. You're a poor excuse for an ogre if you can't smell her at this range.'

'Don't be angry, Muzzer,' whimpered the giant. 'The tree made me bang my nose. It hurts. I can't sniff children with a hurting nose, Muzzer.'

'Serves you right. Must you bleed like that? It's annoying. And stop calling me Mother.'

'But you *are* my muzzer. You said that was what you wanted – a dear little child to call you Muzzer. Don't be sad and lonely – you have me and Gubbins and—'

'You are *not* a dear little child,' the woman interrupted. 'Never were. Hideous then, worse now. You look like a badly grown turnip, and as for Gubbins . . . *what's that?*'

She pointed with the tip of her umbrella at something lying on the ground. As the giant picked it up and handed it to her, Pip recognized it. All the children at Sunny Bay wore the same shoes – the sort that slip on and off without the fuss of laces – known at the orphanage as slinkers. Flora, wherever she was, was short of a slinker.

'Aha!' Holding it up between finger and thumb, the woman sniffed. 'It will do. This is a job for Gubbins. The brute has a nose like a shark scenting blood. Wherever she's hiding, he'll sniff her out.'

'What about me, Muzzer?' asked the giant. 'What should I do?'

'You'll do as you're told,' said his mother briskly. 'The girl will probably try to get back to the road. Follow the tracks the way we came, and keep watch. Make sure you stay out of sight. If they come looking for her, I don't trust you not to put your clodhopper of a foot in it and give our plans away.'

'I won't give anything away,' promised the giant. 'Er . . . what *are* our plans, Muzzer?'

'Too clever for a bean brain like yours to understand,' said the woman. 'All you have to remember is the one rule.'

'Muzzer knows best,' chanted her son, obediently.

'I have waited a long time.' Pocketing Flora's slinker, the woman shook out the folds of her umbrella. 'But it won't be long now. I shall have my revenge. Miss Prim-Prunes Watkyns thinks it's safe to forget – that I'm gone and far away. But broken promises come home to roost. Like bats do.'

The lady stalked through the gap in the yew tree and was gone. With a mournful sigh, her overgrown son wiped his nose on a handful of leaves then set off back towards the road. Pip held his breath as he shuffled close by, muttering to himself. 'Muzzer knows best. Who knows best? Muzzer does . . .'

When there was nothing to be heard but birdsong and

the whisper of leaves in the breeze, Pip came out from behind his bush and inspected the car.

The rear door on the passenger side was hanging off its hinges. Flora must have scrambled out when they hit the tree and gone . . . where? Pip looked around, not daring to call out for her.

Something dropped into the carpet of yew needles at his feet. Flora's other slinker.

Pip tipped his head back, blinking upwards. 'Flora?'

Flora's legs appeared through the branches, followed by the rest of her.

'Are you all right?' Pip looked at her bare feet, torn pinafore and the bird's nest of twigs in her hair. 'We can't stay here. She's sending somebody to sniff you out. He's called Gubbins and he's got the nose of a shark. You'd better try not to smell. We can't go back to the road, either – that giant person is there, watching.'

Where, then? Flora bent to rescue her slinker from the puppy, who had pounced on it. He licked her face, then something – a rustling in the ferns – caught his attention. Tumbling over his own barks, he dived through the split in the old yew tree. The barks grew fainter.

No . . . come back! Flora was on her feet.

'We don't want to go that way,' Pip warned her. '*She* went that way!'

Flora didn't look back. *We have to go after him. He's too little to be all by himself. He needs us.* She was gone, disappearing between the twin gateposts of the Only Yew.

Pip hesitated. Not for long. 'Flora . . . wait for me!'

So it was that two children and a dog passed through a gateway, out of one world and into another, not knowing what they were doing, where they were going, or what they were leaving behind.

CHAPTER 6

Miss Watkyns sat at her desk, not quite as crisp and upright as before. There was a sharp crease between her brows and a loop of dark hair, threaded with silver, had escaped from its pins.

'That boy has always been trouble.' Mr Gribblestone, the schoolmaster, had spidery legs and a stomach that looked as if he might have recently swallowed a melon.

'You're too hard on him, Mr Gribblestone,' objected Miss Scadging. 'Pip had an unlucky start in life.'

'This is an orphanage,' Mr Gribblestone reminded her, stroking his moustache as if it were a small furry animal.

'*All* the children have had unlucky starts – or they wouldn't be here. They are not all such hopeless cases as Pip. He is a very bad influence on poor little Flora.'

'I wouldn't be so sure of that,' retorted Miss Scadging. 'Don't you know better than to trust a child with blue eyes and dimples? Flora eggs him on.'

'How?' demanded Mr Gribblestone. 'When she can't talk?'

'Can't talk or *won't* talk?' said Miss Scadging thoughtfully. 'There's no such thing as a hopeless case, Mr Gribblestone. Plenty of kindness and custard, and those children will turn out right in the end. Even the hairiest caterpillar has a butterfly inside.'

'In the old days,' remarked Mr Gribblestone, 'Master Pip would have been locked in the pigeon loft until he changed his ways.'

'I don't want to think about the old days!' Miss Scadging gave him a fierce look. 'They're over and done with. We were all Sunny Bay orphans once, Mr Gribblestone. Have you forgotten what it was like in Mr Bunphatt's time, before Miss Watkyns took charge? This was a house of darkness and misery. You were only an infant, but I remember the tears, the beatings, the hunger . . .'

She was interrupted by the tramp of heavy boots in the corridor. Captain Vanderdecken stood in the doorway with two of his crew. They clicked their heels and bowed. Miss Watkyns looked up with hope in her eyes.

'Sorry, ma'am.' The Captain was gruff. 'No trace of them. Squashed fruit and wheel marks by the front gates. There's a car gone off the road, into the woods. The vehicle was stolen, according to PC Trubshaw – taken from the village this very morning. My men searched the area.' He gestured at the pair of elderly sailors standing to attention behind him. 'Mr Plankton, Mr Halibut – speak up and tell Miss Watkyns what you found.'

'No bodies, ma'am,' Mr Plankton reassured her. 'Dead or alive.'

'Or anywhere in between,' added Mr Halibut helpfully. 'Just this, ma'am.' Unwrapping a very small object from the folds of his pocket handkerchief, he placed it on the desk in front of her. A sugared violet.

Miss Watkyns stared at the sweet. The colour drained out

of her face, as if she had glimpsed a ghost.

'I am to blame for this,' sighed Captain Vanderdecken. 'I raised my voice to those children. I may have made threats. Keelhauling. Sharks. I never meant to frighten the poor little things into running away.'

'I've heard things about Wyke Wood,' said Mr Plankton, shaking his head.

'Folks have seen things . . .' agreed Mr Halibut.

The Captain frowned. 'Tall tales! You can't expect a sensible woman like Miss Watkyns to believe in stories!'

'On the contrary, Captain,' said Miss Watkyns. 'It is the sensible people who *do* believe in stories. We may pretend that we don't, to make the world seem a safer place. In our hearts, we know better.'

Later, when she was alone, Miss Watkyns sat unmoving, seeing only her own memories. She sat for so long that the goldfish dared to give up its clockwise circles and go the other way. Rousing herself at last, she raised her eyes to a piece of needlework in a frame upon the wall. Letters had been carefully stitched in coloured thread.

HOME IS WHERE THE HEART IS

Pushing back her chair and crossing to the fireplace, Miss Watkyns looked into the mirror hanging on the wall. She tidied her hair then lingered, gazing deep, deep into the glass. Her reflection rippled, looking back at her with an expression that was not her own.

'Don't!' Miss Watkyns spoke out loud. 'Stop it. What happened . . . it's in the past. These children have done you no harm. Let them be. Do you hear me?'

A peal of what might have been laughter rang out close by. Miss Watkyns caught her breath. *Only a gull. Pull yourself together, Felicia Watkyns.*

Turning her back on the mirror, she noticed the goldfish's change of direction.

'I am disappointed in you, Heinrich Cornelius,' she said sternly. 'The forces of darkness may be stirring – is that any reason to let our standards slip?'

In which there is a strong smell of cinnamon. Pip and Flora meet a large animal, an old friend and some badly behaved wobsers. Flora surprises everybody, including herself, and somebody makes purple jelly.

CHAPTER 7

'The good thing about being out *here*,' said Pip, trying to be cheerful, 'is that there aren't any rules.'

Or any meals. The other orphans would be tucking into their picnic on Puffin Island by now. Flora's insides were so hungry, they hurt. Her mouth felt dry and tight with thirst; her bare foot was bruised and prickled. *I don't want to walk any more.* She sank down on to a fallen tree trunk, gathering up the puppy. *We don't even know where we're going.* Alone in her nursery, she had read stories about children who got lost in the woods and came to sad, bad ends.

Pip had never even seen a book until he arrived at Sunny

Bay – the only stories he knew were the ones Miss Scadging read to the orphans on rainy afternoons – but he could feel Flora's mood. He looked at the puppy on her lap. 'It's his fault we're lost.'

The little dog had led the children a merry dance through the trees, deaf to Pip's whistles. What was he chasing? Pip was sure he saw something like a furry snake, and Flora thought she saw a rabbit with antlers. He had come back to them at last, bright-eyed and bedraggled.

'He needs a name,' decided Pip. 'Maybe then he'd learn to come when he's called.'

Neither of them knew much about the naming of dogs.

Algernon? Bonaparte? Caractacus? wondered Flora. *Zebediah?*

'We could just call him Dog,' suggested Pip, who had spent most of his life answering to shouts of *Oi, boy!*

Flora shook her cloud of hair.

Pip thought of the animals he had known in the circus. Fifi and Lulu, the performing poodles – that wouldn't do. The ponies had all had names like Dancer, Misty and Princess. No . . .

Then he remembered the Beast who had saved him from his father that day in the circus ring. She deserved to be remembered. 'What about Tiger?'

Flora frowned. *He's the wrong colour; he doesn't have any stripes. He looks more like a Panda . . .* She could feel the words jostling in her throat. To her surprise, here in the muffled quiet of the wood, they almost escaped. Almost, but not quite.

'Tiger!' called Pip. 'Here, Tiger!'

The puppy's ears twitched. He jumped off the log and went to sit at Pip's feet, tail wagging.

'See?' said Pip.

But Flora wasn't listening. Head tilted, she was sniffing. What was that smell? It made her think of Christmas. *Plum pudding . . . spiced punch . . . cinnamon buns . . .*

Tiger was on his feet, stiff-legged and whining.

Did you hear that?

Shuffling. The crackle of leaves. *Flip flop, flip flop . . .* coming closer. Flora slid down behind her tree trunk, lying flat in the bracken, eyes wide and watchful. Scooping up Tiger, Pip jumped the log and flattened himself beside her.

He could hear the thud of his heart – or was it Flora's? Tiger was squirming, yapping, growling.

Sssh! Desperately, they tried to hush him.

Something had come out from between the trees. The air was heavy with the scent of spice. As the puppy wriggled free, a small strangled cry escaped from Flora.

Huff . . . huffff . . . The sound of heavy breathing. A shape loomed over them – tall on two legs, hulking and shaggy.

Pip couldn't look. In his mind he saw his father towering over him, eyes bulging, fists clenched with rage. He did what he had always done. Curling into a ball like a frightened hedgehog, he squeezed his eyes tight shut and hoped that the darkness would swallow him up.

CHAPTER 8

The lady sat combing out her blackcurrant hair. Flames spat in the grate. As she stretched out her legs, firelight flickered on her purple stockings. Something croaked in the shadows.

'You can be quiet, Mr B,' snapped the woman. 'Have you forgotten the rules? No speaking until you're spoken to.'

As the door opened, somebody very tall squeezed through the gap. Pulling forward a chair, he folded himself into it – the ceiling was too low for him to stand up.

'I brought you the berries, Muzzer. I picked them oh so carefully – no squashing – and didn't eat any. Are they for supper, Muzzer?'

'Fool,' said his mother. 'They're Deadly Nightshade.' She took the basket from him. 'Such a pretty colour . . . I shall make a beautiful purple jelly. It will show me what I want to see.'

The giant looked around him. 'Where is Gubbins?'

'I sent him after the girl. He will find her, and he will bring her to me.'

'Why do you want her, Muzzer? She's just a little girl. Sweet and juicy, I expect,' added the giant wistfully.

'I need her.' The woman's fingers curled for a moment into something like claws. 'She will be my instrument of revenge.'

Her son rubbed his still-swollen nose. 'Thinking of children does make me so horribly, hurtingly hungry.'

'Stop dribbling,' ordered the woman. 'There's turnip soup.'

'I'm terribly tired of turnip,' sighed the giant. 'Turnips don't have bones. Will I ever have bones again? You said I would, Muzzer. You promised.'

'Poor foozelum!' She patted his hand. 'Do as I say, and

the day will come when you may have as many bones as you like.'

'Yes, Muzzer,' said her son obediently. 'Muzzer will make everything right. Nobody is as clever as Muzzer.'

'Lump-head,' said his mother.

CHAPTER 9

Pip, it's all right. Flora's hand was on his shoulder, shaking him. *Pip, open your eyes. Look!* Slowly, cautiously, Pip uncurled.

On the other side of the fallen log stood a large animal. Small round ears, button eyes, thick fur gleaming like newly shelled chestnuts. It had dropped down on all fours and Tiger was frisking around it, tail wagging. As Pip stared, the beast tucked its nose between its hairy front paws and did a neat forward roll. A bear.

It's difficult to stay scared of anything that smells of cinnamon buns and turns somersaults. As Flora climbed over the log the creature ambled towards her, butting her gently in the stomach. Slowly, holding her breath, she reached out a hand.

The bear seemed to enjoy being petted. It stood with its eyes half-closed, huffing and rumbling with pleasure, while Pip scratched its ears and Flora buried her face in its shaggy neck. When it had at last had enough, it shook itself, filling the air with the scent of spice, then turned another row of somersaults. Pip let out a whoop and copied it, following up with a cartwheel and a backflip. He had never shown off his circus tricks at Sunny Bay. The old days were over; he didn't want to think about them. Like Flora, he had stuffed the past into a box at the back of his mind and shut the lid on it – but out here, in the woods, it all seemed too far away to matter.

The bear finished scratching itself against the knobbled bark of a cork oak and lumbered off between the trees, pausing to look over its shoulder at the children, as if to say *Well? Are you coming?*

'We might as well go with it,' said Pip. 'Bears have to eat, don't they? Maybe it will lead us to some food.'

Pip was used to snatching whatever crumb or crust came his way. Flora, in her lonely nursery, had grown up with maids and a cook and regular meals on fine china plates. She didn't miss any of that – but it seemed a very long time since the bowls of treacle porridge and hot buttered toast that started the day at Sunny Bay. And being lost in a wood with a friendly bear is better than being lost in a wood without one.

She started forward after Pip but she was limping. As yet another holly leaf dug its prickles into her heel she winced. Balancing on one leg, she cradled her bare foot.

It hurts . . .

Pip looked thoughtfully at the bear's broad back. 'Do you suppose you could ride it?'

Among the toys in Flora's nursery had been a rocking horse, with dappled paint and a beautiful flowing mane and tail. With nothing else to do, Flora had spent long hours rocking on imaginary journeys. How different could it be? She nodded.

The bear stood patiently while Pip gave Flora a leg up. It

was so wide around the middle, her legs stuck out to either side.

'My mother rode bareback in the circus,' said Pip as the bear shifted and Flora almost toppled off. 'Bears have loads more fur to hang on to than ponies do. Here, you had better take Tiger.' He handed the puppy up to her. 'He'll only run off and get lost again.'

The bear seemed to know where it was going, shambling along at an easy pace. Birds twittered. The afternoon sun trickled like warm syrup between the leaves above their heads. As Flora breathed in the smell of cinnamon buns and grew accustomed to the rhythmic sway of the shaggy shoulders, she forgot about being hungry and thirsty and lost. Something new and unexpected was happening to her . . . Flora was enjoying herself.

They had been travelling for a while when the bear came to a sudden stop. Raising its muzzle, it snuffed the air then set off again at a lolloping canter. Pip was just in time to catch Tiger as he tumbled off. Flora hung on, crouched low over the bear's shoulders. As the world flashed past her, she caught a glimpse of something familiar: a small person with a round face and round eyes, his mouth a round circle of surprise.

Gorbo!

CHAPTER 10

'Jump, Miss Flora!' Gorbo's arms were flailing wildly. 'Get off that bear! Be—'

Be what? Flora didn't hear the rest; her ears were full of the crash and splinter of the bear's mad charge. *Ummph!* As it slithered to a sudden halt, she lost her grip and slid to the ground. The bear was up on its back legs, grunting and scraping with its claws at the bark of a tree.

Pip reached Flora's side, panting. 'What's it doing? What's that noise?'

The tree was humming. As the hum grew louder, out streamed a plume of something like smoke. Buzzing, angry smoke, striped black and yellow.

Bees! Hundreds of them.

Flora was already on her feet and running, shielding her face with her arms. Clutching Tiger, Pip went after her. They kept going, as far away as possible from the cloud of furious bees, until something stretched across their path brought them crashing to the ground.

'String,' said Pip. 'What's that doing there?'

'It might be mine,' admitted a familiar voice. 'I seem to be coming a bit undone.'

Gorbo helped them to their feet. He had a bow and a quiver full of arrows slung across his back and was carrying a string bag, half unravelled.

'What in the name of pudding and pie are you two doing out in the woods, galumphing about on a cinnamon bear? Good-natured beasts, most of the time, but the smell of honey drives them crazy. It annoys the bees, when they take without asking, and if you get in the way it can all end in a very ouch-bee-stingly sort of way.'

'Don't the bears get stung?' asked Pip.

Gorbo shook his head. 'Their fur's too thick and they

have specially bee-proof noses. *There* you are, you trouble-some thing!' Winding his lost string, he had found the end of it caught on a bramble bush.

A breeze rippled through the trees; leaves stirred. Tiger picked up a scent of something nearby. He wriggled and yapped in Pip's arms.

'Odd sort of beast you've got there,' remarked Gorbo. 'It looks like a badly made rabbit.'

A sound came from Flora. It sounded very like an escaped giggle.

'He's a dog,' said Pip.

'What?' Gorbo looked alarmed. 'No, that's not right. I don't know much, but I know what dogs are: great big things with lollopy legs and long snappy snouts full of knife teeth!'

'That's a different sort,' explained Pip. 'Dogs come in different sizes, Gorbo. Like . . . like pieces of string. His name's Tiger – and he's our friend.'

'Oh, well, in *that* case . . .' Gorbo's face cleared. 'Any friend of yours is a friend of Gorbo's. Does he like pancakes?'

Pancakes! Oh! Flora's eyes were full of longing.

'We all like pancakes,' said Pip. 'We've had nothing to eat since breakfast.'

Gorbo looked shocked. 'That's bad. "Full stomach, brave heart", as my mother used to say. "Never, ever set forth on an adventure without packing a pie, my son, in case of emergencies." I'm afraid you're too late for the pie – it's inside me – but I do have some pancakes left.' Rummaging in what was left of his string bag, which seemed to be mostly full of more string, he pulled out some flat, floppy things. 'Cooking's not my best thing; I haven't found out what *is*, to be honest – although my Aunt Flumper does say that I have a rare and remarkable talent for being a gormless globular good-for-nothing gump.'

Gorbo's pancakes were a bit leathery, but they were flavoured with sea salt and wild thyme and the children were much too hungry to be fussy.

'It does seem a very peculiar thing,' observed Gorbo as they ate, 'that the wonderfully wise Miss Watkyns should let you be out here on your own, without so much as a slice of pie between you, chasing about on honey-mad bears and getting into who-knows-what sort of trouble. There haven't been any dragons seen in these parts for a while and the last of the ogres has been dealt with, but there's always a risk of wobsers – and supposing you had been captured by Kelps?'

'What's a Kelp?' asked Pip with his mouth full.

'Bad, mostly. They live *that* way,' Gorbo waved a hand. 'Nobody's seen one this side of the river for a very long time, and a good thing too. I've never met one – and never want to – but everyone knows the stories. "Beware the Kelps, they are not nice. They dine on babies boiled with rice . . ." There's more,' added Gorbo darkly, 'but I don't want to put you off your pancake. Kelps aren't friendly and Snergs don't like them: that's how it is and that's how it's always been.'

'Supposing we did meet one,' wondered Pip, swallowing the last crumbs of his pancake, 'How would we know? What do they look like?'

'Long and noodle-y, like your human sort,' said Gorbo. '*Not* like a Snerg. Easy to know a Snerg when you meet one. No taller than we ought to be and nearly always cheerful. Except when we're hungry. And that's a bit of a worry . . .' Feeding the last pancake to Tiger, who had already swallowed three and was swelling up into a much happier puppy, Gorbo peered into his string bag. 'I'd reckoned on having enough food to last until I got home, but now I see that I must get you two back to Miss Watkyns. That makes one long journey plus three stomachs . . .' Counting on his fingers, Gorbo looked at Tiger. 'Plus one more, plus no food left. That's the wrong sort of sum. It doesn't come out properly.'

Pip and Flora met each other's eyes, the same thought in both their heads.

'We don't want to go back to Sunny Bay,' announced Pip. Flora shook her head, making the dried leaves rustle in her curls. 'We want to come with you, Gorbo.'

'I don't know about that,' Gorbo scratched his head. 'What would Miss Watkyns say?'

'Why should she care?' said Pip. 'She doesn't want us – we just make her cross. They all went on a picnic without us. They left us behind. On purpose.'

Gorbo looked upset. 'But Miss Watkyns is wise and kind.'

Pip shook his head. 'Not if you break her rules, she's not. She sent *you* away, didn't she? She'll be glad to be rid of us too. Please, Gorbo. We want to see where you live – and meet some more Snergs.'

With two pairs of pleading eyes fixed upon him, Gorbo floundered.

'The town of the Snergs is a very marvellous place,' he admitted. 'And the Queen's feasts are the marvellous-est thing of all. There will be one tonight . . .' His face clouded. 'But the Queen is not happy with poor Gorbo. I shall be uninvited.'

'Why?'

Gorbo sighed. 'There was a spot of bother at the last feast: it was in honour of Her Majesty's 373rd-and-three-quarters birthday. I don't *exactly* remember what happened. There may have been some dancing. It may have been on the table. I *may* have turned a few cartwheels. There may have been some *slippage*. There's a definite possibility that I landed bang in the middle of Her Majesty's birthday cake. It was a lucky thing the candles hadn't been lit, but there was a good deal of jam involved. My breeches were definitely *squelchy*. Next to pie, cake is what Her Majesty likes best and this one had been constructed in her own likeness by the Head Pudding Fellow. Cake,' observed Gorbo, 'does not look quite the same after someone has sat in it. The Queen sent me away after that.' He heaved a heart-rending sigh. 'And now Miss Watkyns has sent me away too. The Queen will hear about it and I shall be uninvited to all the feasts for the next hundred years, as sure as wobsers have teeth.'

'Let us come with you,' wheedled Pip, 'and we'll explain it was our fault that Miss Watkyns sent you away.'

Gorbo hesitated. 'The Snergs would like to see you; they are very fond of visitors. And the Queen will be glad to have news of her good friend, Miss Watkyns.'

'Has Miss Watkyns met the Queen?' Pip was surprised.

'Oh, well, it was a long time ago,' said Gorbo vaguely. Changing the subject, he added, 'Perhaps if I take the Queen a present of some honeycomb, it will sweeten her mood . . . if that bear hasn't gobbled the lot.'

'What about the bees?' asked Pip. 'Won't you get stung?'

'I shall ask them politely – and anyway Snergs have very thick skin,' said Gorbo cheerfully. 'But you two had better stay here. If you don't mind my saying so, you do smell rather of cinnamon – the bees might mistake you for a bear. If anything happens – anything uncomfortable – do this . . .' He cupped his hands around his mouth. '. . . *ooo-k-uck* . . . *ooo-k-uck* . . . *ooo-k-uck* . . . It's the call of the discombobulated cuckoo. Any trouble, just call and I'll come.'

The children watched him go, blending back into the undergrowth in his green waistcoat and tattered brown breeches.

'I'm glad we found him,' said Pip.

It will be all right now, agreed Flora.

Gorbo was perhaps not the most grown up of the grown-ups they knew – in height or any other way – but they trusted him to take care of things.

Miss Watkyns, had anybody asked her, might have warned them against putting too much trust in a Snerg as famously scatterbrained as Gorbo.

Miss Watkyns might have been right.

CHAPTER 11

'Ow!'

Pip had been lying on his stomach, idly watching a line of ants carry away the last of the pancake crumbs. At Flora's yelp he looked up, startled.

'Flora, did you just *say* something?' He broke off, staring.

Flora had been sitting with her back against a tree trunk, picking splinters out of her bare foot. Now, grimacing with pain and shock, she was fighting off a creature that hung by its curly tail from the branch above her head. Dangling like a swollen pink balloon, bald and bristly with bulging fish-eyes, it was yanking at Flora's hair with its long, toothed beak.

'Hey, get *off* her!' Scrambling to his feet, Pip looked around him for a weapon. Snatching up a stick, he swiped at the creature. 'Get *off*!'

Tiger, comfortably full of pancake, had been dozing in a patch of sunlight. Wide awake now, he hurled himself at the tree. He was on his back legs, yapping and snapping when another pink blob swung down, curled its tail around his neck and lifted him off the ground.

Flora let out a howl of fury and made a wild grab, catching hold of the puppy's tail just as the rest of him disappeared up into the leaves. Poor Tiger whined, feeling uncomfortably stretched as a fierce beak at one end yanked him upwards and Flora at the other end tugged him down. It was looking as if the beak would win the tug-of-war – or Tiger would be pulled into two halves – when Pip cupped his hands to his mouth.

'*Ooo-k-uck . . . ooo-k-uck . . . ooo-k-uck . . .*'

Suddenly there were pink blobs everywhere, swarming down tree trunks on sticky webbed feet, beaks clicking.

'*Ooo-k-uck . . . ooo-k-uck . . .*'

As Flora clung desperately to Tiger's tail, Pip lashed out

with his stick. The creatures made horrible gurgling sounds, like broken plumbing, but it was no use: there were too many of them.

As an especially bloated blob dropped to the ground in front of Pip, whipping its tail around his ankle and tripping him, an arrow flew with a *phwut!* through the air.

'Two twos: four,' shouted Gorbo's voice. 'Three threes: nine.'

The blobs froze, seeming to shrivel slightly.

'Four fours: sixteen!' Gorbo came crashing through the bracken in a breathless rush.

The blobs glugged, rolling their jellied eyes. Pip managed to pull his foot free; the tail around Tiger's neck loosened its grip.

'Five fives: twenty-five,' panted Gorbo. 'Be gone, wobsers – or I'll mathematize the lot of you! Six sixes: thirty-six. Seven sevens: er . . . forty . . . um . . . forty-something. Forty . . . seven . . . ?'

At Gorbo's mistake, the wobsers recovered. There were more of them than ever now, pouring out of the treetops, burbling triumphantly.

'Eight eights,' yelled Gorbo. 'Um . . . um . . .'

'Sixty-four!' It was Flora, the words torn out of her as wobser beaks ripped at her hair. 'Nine nines: eighty-one. Get *off* me, you repulsive, revolting, disgusting, detestable, preposterous pink *pudding*! Ten tens: too easy. Eleven elevens: one hundred and twenty-one! Leave Tiger *alone*, he's smaller than you, you pusillanimous puffed-up, pop-eyed pig! Twelve twelves: one hundred and forty-four! Thirteen thirteens . . . wait, I can do it . . . one hundred and sixty-nine!'

This was too much for the wobsers. Bubbling and squealing like spiteful steam kettles, they turned tail and scuttled back up into the trees.

'Flora!' Pip was staring at her. 'Did you hear what you just *did*?'

But Flora, hunching up one shoulder, had disappeared behind her hair. She wasn't sure what had happened; she hadn't been expecting it. The words had exploded out of her in something like an enormous sneeze.

'And a good thing too!' Gorbo straightened his cap, very much relieved. 'That's the thing about wobsers. Nobody knows why, but they can't stand multiplication. The trouble is, when you have to remember your sums in a hurry, they don't always come out right. We might have found ourselves in a pretty pickle if Miss Flora hadn't turned out to be so clever.'

Holding tight on to Tiger, Flora gave a little wordless shake of the head. Her governess had believed in tests: history, geography, spelling and arithmetic. If you spend years of your life having tests every day and twice on Mondays, you can't help knowing stuff. She did not say so. The sound of her own voice, after so long, had startled her just as much as it had upset the wobsers.

Pip too was silent. At Sunny Bay, Mr Gribblestone had done his best to teach him some arithmetic. Pip had stared blankly at even the simplest of sums. Why did any of it matter? There was always something more interesting to think about. Now, for the first time ever, he began to see that maybe, when you were least expecting it, all that stuff in lessons might turn out useful after all.

'If I had shot a little straighter, we could have cooked one.' Gorbo pulled his arrow out of the tree trunk where it had stuck. 'Although I can't pretend they taste very nice – rubbery and a bit slimy. I've never seen so many, not all at once.'

'There was only one to start with,' said Pip. 'It was pulling Flora's hair. Then a second one arrived and was trying to steal Tiger, so I thought I'd better call you like you said – then suddenly they were everywhere. Gorbo, what's wrong?'

Gorbo had clapped one hand to his mouth, using the other to thump himself on the head.

'Gorbo, you clonk-headed, ridonculous, knobble-pated nitwit,' he insulted himself. 'Aunt Flumper was quite right; you are a disgrace to the race of Snerg! You *deserve* to be nibbled to death by wobsers, your bones crunched, your blood slurped, your tough bits chewed and spat out . . .'

He was on his knees, still buffeting himself. The children looked at him in concern.

'Gorbo, please stop,' begged Pip. 'Whatever is the matter?'

Gorbo swallowed a sob. 'It was me. I told you to use that signal!'

'The call of the discombobulated cuckoo?' Pip cupped his hands to his mouth. '*Ooo-k-uk—*'

'Don't! Don't do it, Master Pip,' Gorbo beseeched him tearfully. 'Not unless you want to bring them all back! I forgot – blithering buffle-brained nincompoop of a Snerg – discombobulated cuckoos are a wobser's favourite food! I as good as got you guzzled up. Whatever would Miss Watkyns say? I am not a proper person to be looking after innocent children. It is time to be a sensible Snerg, for once in my life, and take you straight back to Sunny Bay!'

Pip frowned. 'Does Miss Watkyns *know* about wobsers? Because if she does – why did she say there's no such thing?'

'Miss Watkyns is a most excellent lady,' said Gorbo firmly. 'I'm sure she had very good reasons.'

'It would be her fault if we *did* get eaten by wobsers,' declared Pip. 'She should have warned us about them. Not that she cares – not one bit! Don't send us back, Gorbo. Not yet. We won't go, will we, Flora?'

Behind her hair, Flora shook her head.

'If you try to make us,' said Pip, cupping his hands to his mouth, 'I'll do it again. I'll make the call of the discom-what's-you-lated cuckoo . . .'

'No, don't do that!' begged Gorbo. 'Or we'll be stuck here

doing mathematical gymnasticals until our heads spin. Won't you be sensible Noodlings and—'

'We'll be very sensible,' promised Pip, '*if* you take us to see the Snergs.'

Gorbo gave up.

'Well, if that's how it is . . .' he sighed. Shouldering his bow, he pulled his cap down over his ears. 'Heigh-ho then, and off we go – off to the Land of the Snergs.'

They had not gone far before the bear came slouching back to them, rather sticky about the muzzle, butting at their legs and rolling on the ground to get their attention.

'If you've got nothing better to do than turn skitterwitted somersaults,' Gorbo told it sternly, 'you may as well make yourself useful and carry a passenger.'

As the little band of travellers set off, none of them noticed a single green eye watching them through the ferns – especially watching Flora, with her one missing shoe.

CHAPTER 12

'Snergs! How I hate them! Bobbing about like little rays of sunshine, being so stupidly helpful and friendly. Must they always be so cheerful? It makes me feel ill.'

The woman's voice was as bitter as the nightshade jelly she had mixed. She had poured it into a bowl made from a polished skull. It was not quite set. As she tilted the bowl, the surface rippled. The woman frowned, twisting a lock of her elderberry hair.

'Can you see them, Muzzer?' Her gangling son stood at her shoulder, rubbing his bruised nose.

'Gorbo, that fool, is taking them to the Snergs.' She gave

the skull bowl an irritated shake.

'Don't make me go there, Muzzer,' whimpered the giant. 'They have birds. Big birds. Snappy beaks, fierce feet.'

'I've known cucumbers with more courage than you,' remarked his mother. 'Did I deserve such a son? A head full of rubble and less backbone than boiled broccoli. I don't need your help. Gubbins is close behind them.'

'Bruzzer Gubbins doesn't always do as you tell him. He's a naughty boy. Not like me,' said the ogre virtuously. 'I'm your good boy.' He reached out his ham of a fist to give her a clumsy pat but she pushed him away.'

'I can't see,' she complained. 'You're blocking the light, lump. I want to see the girl. Soon I shall have her in my power . . . then it begins.'

'And when it's finished, then I can eat bones again,' said the ogre happily. 'Crunchy on the outside, melty on the inside. I can, can't I, Muzzer?'

'As many as you like, my son.' The woman gazed into the purple depths of her jelly, lips curling as it showed her a house by the sea – a large building with tall chimneys and high iron gates, guarded by two rowan trees.

'You think you can keep me out with your rowan and your rosemary,' she murmured to someone who was not there. 'But I am cleverer than that. You'll see. Flames and black smoke will blot out the sun at Sunny Bay, until all the memories are nothing but ash, blowing on the wind . . .'

In which the travellers arrive
at the Town of the Snergs and
Gorbo receives an Un-invitation.
The Queen holds a feast, with the proper
amount of pie, song and standing on
heads, and the adventure seems to
be almost over — until Tiger finds
something to chase through
the Twisted Trees . . .

CHAPTER 13

Rather than chopping and flattening their woodland home, Snergs build their houses in the trees, between the trees and around the trees. The first you know of it, approaching from afar, is the tinkling of wind bells and the waterfall of colour from the window boxes and hanging baskets high up in the branches. Then you might notice the birds' nests perched on twisting chimney pots, high red roofs and cheerfully painted doorways hidden behind the leaves, with winding wooden staircases in unexpected places.

'Here we are,' said Gorbo, his face brightening. 'Journeys

are all very well, but the best ones always bring you home where everything's where you left it, your furniture's pleased to see you and there's plenty of string.'

Gorbo's return caused something of a stir. No sooner was he spotted than the cry went up . . .

'Well, I'll be flabbered! If it isn't that old bag of nonsense, Gorbo!'

'Woo-hoo, Gorbo! Back again so soon?'

'Just in time for tonight's feast – isn't that just like Gorbo!'

'Does the Queen know he's back?'

The Snerg way of greeting any friend they haven't seen for more than about ten minutes is to cross wrists, join hands and whirl around in circles. This leads to very energetic gatherings and some danger to passers-by. As more and more of them came thronging to welcome Gorbo they seized on Pip and Flora too, spinning them until they were breathless and giddy. Blinking away their dizziness, they looked about them at the merry higgledy-piggledy-ness that is a town of Snergs.

Snergs are great builders. As their families grow (or their collections of string, jam, interesting pebbles or may-be-useful-one-day stuff), they put out extensions. If there is no room on the ground floor, they build it higher up. Sometimes an extension arching out from a first, second or third storey will bump into another one belonging to the house opposite, or next door, forming a network of bridges and convenient passageways for friendly neighbours. Right now, there seemed to be a Snerg in every doorway, at every window and hanging over every balcony.

'Gorbo? What foolishness are you up to now?' A very old Snerg, tending his window box high in a silver birch tree, waved his watering can at Gorbo. 'What have you brought with you?' He peered at Flora. 'Her legs are too long. Not a Kelp, is she?'

'*Kelp . . . Kelp . . .*'

The whisper rustled through the town as the Snergs drew back.

'Of course she's not a Kelp,' said Gorbo crossly. 'These are friends of mine from Sunny Bay. They belong to Miss Watkyns – so mind what you say!'

'*Miss Watkyns . . . Miss Watkyns . . .*'

This time, the whisper was respectful.

'We don't *belong* to her, exactly,' said Pip. 'We don't belong anywhere, to anybody.'

'Hey, Gorbo!' A Snerg with a wide grin, armed with hammer and saw, sat perched on the roof gable she had been mending. 'Did you see her, then: the wise Watkyns? Has she made a sensible Snerg out of you?'

'*Miss* Watkyns to you – and of course I saw her. We're very good friends, she and I,' declared Gorbo, not quite truthfully.

'So why have you come back? And does she know that you have stolen two of her half-Noodles?'

'I haven't *stolen* them,' retorted Gorbo. 'They have come to visit the Queen. This noble bear has carried them a long way.'

At the side of the town's long main street was a small stall loaded with baskets of apples. Behind it sat a rosy-cheeked Snerg, looking much like an apple herself.

'An apple for the bear, if you please, Miss Mopsa.' Reaching into the pocket of his breeches, Gorbo brought out a handful of shells gathered from the beach at Sunny Bay. As the Snerg picked out her favourites, Gorbo's eye fell upon some little fruit pies.

'One for the bear, one for each of my friends – don't forget the little hairy one – and then there's me. That makes five which is a very odd, spiky sort of a number, so we'll have two each and make it a nice round ten.'

'Ten pies will cost more shells than I need,' said Mopsa. 'Tell us a tale, Mr Gorbo. Make it a good one and you may have *all* the pies.'

It is a custom among Snergs to pay for their shopping with stories. This makes for long queues on market days, but nobody minds if they have a tale to listen to – and the good thing about stories, unlike money, is that they never run out.

'A tale! A tale!' Small Snerg children swarmed between the bear's legs, seating themselves cross-legged at Gorbo's feet.

'No fidgeting and no squeaking,' Gorbo instructed them. 'Hereby begins the terrible tale of Golithos the Ogre, foul of breath and fierce of fang . . .'

'But Gorbo, you told that one last time,' complained one of the Snerglets.

'And the time before,' said another.

'He always tells it,' said the Snerg on the rooftop, thwacking a nail with her hammer. 'It's the only one he knows.'

'A good story is like good cake – worth tasting more than once,' argued Gorbo, offended.

'I wouldn't mention cake if I were you, Gorbo!' shouted a voice in the crowd. 'Not after what you did to the Queen's!'

There was laughter at this, then a cheer as Gorbo, undaunted, jumped up on to Mopsa's stall and flung out his arms.

'Friends, Snergs, bears – lend me your ears and I shall tell you a new tale: the tale of Bold Gorbo and his adventures beyond the woods, in the Marvellous Land of Miss Watkyns, where the sunlight sparkles on the sea, the dolphins leap and the crabs all walk sideways.'

His audience looked up at him, round-eyed and expectant, but Gorbo got no further. At the sound of a horn being blown the crowd stirred and parted, making space for a square Snerg wearing a tall feather in his cap and an I'm-Important expression on his face.

The Snerg stopped in front of Gorbo.

'Are you Gorbo, of the Badly Built House in the Beech Tree?'

'You know perfectly well that I am,' said Gorbo. 'We've known each other since we were Snerglets, Pompo.'

'That was then,' sniffed Pompo. 'Now I am Her Majesty's most Magniloquent and Mellifluous Messenger. Message for you. Handle with care,' he added, passing Gorbo a flat, rectangular object. 'Icing's not hard.'

It is a habit among Snergs to communicate by biscuit. If you are lucky, the post arrives just as you are getting hungry in between breakfast and lunch; you can read your letters and then eat them. The Queen has trained pastry scribes to write her wishes and requests in beautifully joined-up royal icing. As Gorbo stood looking at his biscuit, there was a sympathetic murmur from the crowd.

'Poor old Gorbo, in trouble already . . .'

'The Queen's Biscuit – that'll be an un-invitation to the feast.'

'Bad luck, Gorbo.'

'She knows I'm back then . . .' Gorbo looked a little anxious.

'Of course she knows. Her Royal Resplendence,' announced Pompo, 'is omnipresent, omniscient – and omnivorous. For those lacking in education,' he went on, with a scornful look at Gorbo, 'that means she *is* every-where, *knows* everything and *eats*—'

'Anything. I know *that*,' retorted Gorbo. 'I'm not as stupid as you think. So you can take your hippopotamonstrous big words, Pompo, and stick them right up your nose!'

Pompo shrugged. 'Anyway,' he said, a bit less haughtily, 'the lookout saw you.'

Shading their eyes against the sunlight dancing through the leaves, everyone looked upwards. In the topmost branches of the tallest tree was a platform made of twigs, like a large bird's nest. On it stood a small figure, peering down at them.

Gorbo looked at his biscuit and sighed. The icing was still runny and some of the letters had dribbled into each other. It didn't matter – he knew what they said.

The Queen's feasts happened whenever she felt like it, which was often. The whole town was invited, except for anyone unlucky enough to have recently displeased Her

Majesty. This being so, it was easier – and saved on biscuits – to send out un-invitations only. This wasn't the first time Gorbo had received one.

Queen Mercy of the Snergs and their Surroundings
does most cordially
NOT invite
Gorbo of the Badly Built House by the Beech Tree
to tonight's feast.
(Usual place. Usual time. Don't be there.)

'You can't come,' said Pompo, rubbing it in. 'But her Quintessential Queenliness wants to see you. She wants to see the Noodles, too. I'm to escort you to the Royal Oak.'

'Now?' asked Gorbo nervously.

'Can't keep her Imperial Impatience waiting,' said Pompo. 'Quick sticks!'

CHAPTER 14

The Queen's palace was built around a high, spreading oak. The spider's web of bridges and passageways running off it, into nearby trees, meant that important people – such as the Chancellor of the Jam Pots or the Chief Ostrich Keeper – could be summoned very quickly when required. Up above, the lookout nest was manned at all times so that the Queen could be kept informed of surprise visits from wobsers, goblins or other unexpected guests. She liked to know that her Snergs were going about their business happily. At the first report of a Snerg in distress – anything from a stubbed toe to a lost shopping list – the emergency services were instantly mobilized to provide good cheer, comfort and cake.

Pompo led them up a great many steps, spiralling around the oak's trunk, then on to a high platform facing heavy double doors. Glancing down at the upturned faces of all the Snergs below, Pip had a nasty moment – a sudden flashback to his days on the circus trapeze. Pompo blew a blast on his horn.

'No need to give us all a headache, Pompo,' remarked a voice from inside. 'You could just knock, like everybody else.'

As the doors swung open, Pompo cleared his throat. 'Your Most Momentous Majesty, Pulchritudinous Potentate and Sesquipedalian Sovereign, Queen Mercy of the Snergs and their Surroundings—'

'Show off,' muttered Gorbo.

'. . . I bring you Gorbo of the Badly Built House by the Beech Tree, two half Noodles and an unidentified Animal.'

Pip and Flora kept close to Gorbo, unsure what to expect. Royalty – even when not very big – can be unpredictable. Within, the air was cool and dappled. The shutters were flung wide but several of the windows had leafy branches growing in through them, one complete with a nest full of squawking baby birds. The Queen sat on an oaken throne, wrapped in a cloak of feathers. Her high crown of polished wood made up for her lack of height. It rose up from her head, carved into the long neck of a bird with a fierce beak and jewelled eyes. As it is not dignified for a Queen to be dangling her legs, her feet rested on a feathered cushion.

Gorbo bowed so low he folded himself almost in half, his clenched fists stacked on top of his head in the Snerg salute. To be polite, Pip and Flora copied him.

'Hail, most Multidimensional Majesty,' said Gorbo respectfully. 'May your shadow ever be a wide one.'

'Gorbo.' The Queen's voice was deep, for a small person. 'You are like an annoying fly that keeps buzzing back. Were you not requested to remove yourself from the Land of the Snergs and give us all a rest from your foolishness?'

'Umm . . .' said Gorbo, still upside down and rather muffled.

Pompo cleared his throat. 'On the 33rd day of the month before the month after the month before last,' he recited, 'you, Gorbo of the Badly Built House by the Beech Tree, were charged with an offence against Her Majesty, Queen Mercy of the Snergs. You were found guilty of being Disorderly at Table and of Damage to Desserts. Henceforward and hereafter to be known as Gorbo the Blunderer, you were sent from this place, never to return – or at least not until her Magnanimous Majesty forgot about it.'

'You must think I have a very short memory,' remarked the Queen. 'You may stand up straight. I cannot have a sensible conversation with the back of a person's head – although in your case, I doubt it will make much difference. Who are your companions?'

'Friends, O Most Quadrilateral Queen.' Gorbo straightened up, rather pink in the cheeks. 'Visiting, from Sunny Bay.'

'Friends of Miss Watkyns are always welcome here.' The Queen looked thoughtfully at her bedraggled, bramble-scratched guests, their clothes shredded and their hair full of leaves and twigs. 'She must have a high opinion of your good sense, Gorbo, to hand two of her young ones into your safekeeping for such a long and perilous journey. Why does this surprise me?'

'A perilous journey indeed, your Royal Robustness,' agreed Gorbo. 'Honey-troubled bears, mad bees, wobsers – I don't know what would have become of them if I hadn't happened to come along . . .' He tailed off, as the Queen's brows snapped together under her wooden crown.

'Two little Noodles wandering in the forest, all alone? Miss Watkyns would never allow it. This smells wrong to me. Gorbo, I know your brain is full of wormholes and earwigs – and I daresay you can't help it, which is why I put up with you – but surely even you would not bring me *runaways*? Did it not enter that woolly head of yours to get these children back where they belong?'

'He tried, your . . . er . . . Queen-ness.' Pip came to Gorbo's defence. 'We wouldn't go. He couldn't make us. And we didn't run away. Not on purpose. We were only in the woods because the purple lady tried to steal Flora—'

'Purple?' The Queen leant forward, her eyes sharp and bright. 'What purple lady?'

'She pretended to be nice,' said Pip. 'But she wasn't. She took Flora and then, when she lost her, she sent somebody called Gubbins to sniff her out.'

'She who wears purple . . .' The Queen frowned, her fingers tapping on the arms of her throne. 'That one has not been seen in these parts for a very long time. And how could she be in Sunny Bay, when the gate is kept closed and she cannot pass through?' Her frown deepened. 'Gorbo, surely not even you would have blundered through the Only Yew and forgotten to close it behind you?'

Gorbo shook his head vigorously. 'No, Your Majestic-alness, I wouldn't . . . I couldn't . . . I didn't . . . I . . .' He faltered and slowly the headshake turned into a nod. 'I may have . . . I . . . I did.' With the Queen's eyes drilling into him, he sank to his knees; he seemed to be melting with guilt. 'I forgot . . .'

'Gorbo, *what have you done?*' The Queen sat back on her throne. 'If the Only Yew stands open, anyone – any*thing* – may pass through it. If trouble comes of this – if harm is done – it will be your fault! I must warn Miss Watkyns and let her know that we have her young ones safe. Pompo, I shall need an ostrich and a rider. I have not heard of this Gubbins. Let us hope that he has lost the scent – I shall post extra lookouts, just in case.'

As Pompo threw open the oak doors, a pile of Snergs fell into the room, all of whom had been trying to peer through the keyhole and listen to Gorbo's telling-off. As they picked themselves up, Tiger suddenly squirmed out of Flora's arms and made a bouncing rush at the feather cushion beneath the Queen's feet. Rudely roused, the cushion removed its head from under its wing. Pip and Flora stared as it rose to its full height, a long way above their heads. Tiger backed off, his tail between his legs, as the bird stamped a large foot and stretched out its long neck, glaring at him with eyes like fierce, long-lashed marbles.

'Restrain that animal!' ordered the Queen. 'Get rid of it. It is harassing Sir Stampensnapper. Gorbo, have you forgotten the penalty for disgruntling an ostrich?'

'No, O Querimonious Queen. Hoisted by the heels and spanked with a wet fish,' mumbled Gorbo, looking very unhappy.

'It's not Gorbo's fault,' said Pip quickly. 'Tiger's only a puppy; he's not very well-trained yet – but he doesn't have anyone to look after him except us.'

Stroking the head of her ostrich, which had subsided into

a hissy heap of feathers at her feet, the Queen gave the children a long, considering look. She could go a long time without blinking; they held their breath.

'You have good hearts, I think,' she said at last. 'Kindness is always welcome here. You have done enough travelling for one day. Tomorrow, my ostrich riders will escort you back to Sunny Bay. Tonight, you are our guests. Pompo, remind me – what is the feast in honour of this time?'

Pompo cleared his throat. 'The Chancellor of the Jam Pots has found his lost socks, Your Majesty.'

'That,' said the Queen, 'is a very poor excuse for a party. Could nobody think of anything better? Never mind the Chancellor's socks. We shall feast in honour of our friends, the half-Noodles, who have come all the way from Sunny Bay to visit us.'

The assembled Snergs clapped and cheered.

'Thank you, Your Marvellous Majesty.' Pip gave his best circus bow; Flora bobbed a curtsey. 'But . . . can Gorbo come?'

Queen Mercy stopped smiling; the clappers and cheerers went quiet.

'Gorbo is un-invited to all feasts until he shows signs of becoming a sedate and sensible Snerg,' pronounced the Queen. 'He can spend the evening cleaning out the ostrich house.'

'Oh, please,' begged Pip. 'Gorbo saved our lives. He rescued us from the wobsers. There were hundreds of them.'

Gorbo blushed. 'It was Miss Flora who knew her times tables,' he pointed out. 'And there wouldn't have been so many wobsers if I hadn't been bumble-brained enough to— *Ow!*' Flora had given him a kick to shut him up.

'*And,*' went on Pip, 'we were starving and Gorbo gave us his very last pancake!'

There was a gasp and a swell of murmuring from the Snergs in the doorway.

'His last pancake! Did you hear that?'

'Gorbo gave them his very *last pancake*!'

Even the Queen looked impressed.

'That was a noble deed,' she conceded. 'Maybe there is hope for you after all, Gorbo. You may come to the feast – but at midnight you must report to the ostrich house for the night watch. If I see your face after midnight, there will be wet fish and spankings. Do you understand?'

'Yes, O Most Marmalade and Magnelephantasmagorical of Majesties!' Gorbo's smile stretched from ear to ear. 'I am ever your most gratitudinous of Snergs and will behave myself most decoraciously for ever after!'

'Hmph,' said the Queen. 'We'll see about that.'

CHAPTER 15

Preparations for the feast were in full swing. Snergs were heaving stools and long wooden tables, lining them up along the street all the way from the Queen's Oak to the market place.

'Flora, look!' Pip clapped his hands. 'We're going to have a picnic after all! This is better than Puffin Island!'

String looped from house to house, flapping scraps of brightly coloured cloth and ribbon. The air was heavy with the smells of happy things to come; behind every window there seemed to be a Snerg stirring or kneading or rolling out pastry.

'Not far to go,' said Gorbo. 'My house is just over there, at the end of those trees.' He pointed at a line of beeches. 'It's a bit falling-down-ish, I'm afraid.'

The children walked on either side of him, with Tiger trotting on the end of a piece of string. The Queen had pardoned him – even ordered a saucer of meat scraps to be brought from the kitchen for him – on condition that he was kept on a lead and not allowed to disgruntle any more ostriches.

Gorbo's house was composed mostly of turrets, piled one on top of another like badly stacked pepperpots, wound tightly around with ivy and a great deal of string. Inside was cheerful, if sawdusty, the walls decorated with little coloured snail shells and polished pebbles and some inky portraits of smiling Snergs.

Flora was just in time to stop Tiger from eating the dry biscuit lying on Gorbo's doormat.

'The voles have been at it already,' remarked Gorbo, inspecting its nibbled edges. He looked at the writing, iced in a spidery hand. 'It's a letter from Aunt Flumper.' And he gave it straight back to Tiger, who swallowed it gratefully.

'Do you live all by yourself?' asked Pip.

Gorbo nodded. 'Just me. Except when a bird falls down the chimney. Sometimes there's a squeazel, but they're not to be trusted. They hide your slippers and leave teeth marks in the cheese. I had a mother and father, once upon a time . . . My mother was one of the Queen's Ostrich Riders.' He waved a hand at the portraits on the wall. 'There she is.'

Pip and Flora peered at the sketch of a Snerg standing with her arm around the neck of an ostrich. Perched on the ostrich's back was a very small Snerglet.

'Is that you, Gorbo?'

Gorbo nodded. 'A remarkable Snerg, my mother.' His face clouded. 'She died winning the Grand Annual Pie-Eating Championship. Choked on a cherry stone in her very last mouthful. We buried her wrapped in pastry – it's what she would have wanted. I take after my father.' He pointed at a wide, smiling Snerg wearing an apron. 'Bombus the Bumbling. He was a baker, until the day he tripped over his rolling pin and fell out of the kitchen.'

'*Can* you fall out of a kitchen?' Pip was doubtful.

'Nothing easier,' Gorbo assured him, 'if it's a long way up

and you haven't got around to building all the walls. My Aunt Flumper took care of me after that. She has a serious mind and likes to live out of town, where it's quieter. She doesn't approve of too much feasting and jollying-about.'

'If you don't have a mother or a father that makes you an orphan. Like us,' said Pip.

'I suppose it does.' Gorbo scratched his head. 'Me, a Norphan: fancy that. It's not so bad – not as long as we do it together. There's a bucket there for washing – don't mind the tadpoles.' He started up his rickety stairs, a number of which were missing. 'I daresay I can find enough clothes for three.'

The children were still wearing their regulation Sunny Bay blue and white uniform. It was the Queen who had suggested – very politely– that they might be more comfortable washed and changed for the feast. Pip, the circus urchin, had never had much to do with soap or hairbrushes but Flora's mother – who had liked to see her daughter smothered in bows and frills – might have had trouble recognizing the tangled ragamuffin with the scraped knees, torn skirt and twiggy hair. Half an hour later, she wouldn't have known her at all.

'Hey, Flora!' Pip grinned at her. 'You've turned into a Snerg!'

So? Adjusting her cap, Flora looked him up and down. *So have you!*

Snergs save time and trouble by wearing the same outfit for every occasion – breeches, tunic and a saucer-shaped cap, all in woodland shades of brown and green. Gorbo's spares were a little baggy on Pip and rather too short for Flora, but they did well enough. Flora's feet were too big for a Snerg, but Gorbo cobbled together some scraps of leather which could be tied around her ankles with string.

'Proper Snergs,' approved Gorbo, inspecting them. 'A bit on the narrow side, mind – and you need to stop growing, Miss Flora – but you'll do.'

As guests of honour, Pip and Flora were given seats at the Queen's table.

'Not you, Gorbo.' Pompo, busy and bossy, pointed at a table so far down the street it was almost around the corner. 'You're down there.'

Without Gorbo at their side the children felt a little

lonely, but they were seated between Mopsa, the apple-seller, and a shy young Snerg named Wilmus.

'Apprentice to the Queen's Own Stringmaker.' Mopsa introduced him. 'He doesn't talk much – and when he does, it's only about string. If he gets too boring, stick a potato in his mouth.'

The Queen herself was lowered through the branches of the Royal Oak, on a special string-powered platform. She sat astride her ostrich, looking very royal in her feathered cloak and tall headdress while the Snergs all rose to their feet, clinking their mead pots, and sang the Snerg Anthem:

Good Queen Mercy comes to town,
Riding on an ostrich.
Hear the Snergs cheer all around,
Let's all have a sandwich!

Food was piled high – on the tables, on the ground, balanced in hammocks hung from the branches. Everybody helped themselves, then helped themselves to more, and more again. Ostriches strutted here and there, snaking out their long necks to pick titbits off people's plates. Nobody argued with the Queen's birds. (Tiger had been left to sleep off his adventures at Gorbo's house, out of the way of temptation.)

Wilmus had pulled a tangle of string out of his pockets and was teaching Flora how to tie knots: the Strangling Snake, the Weaving Worm and the Un-untieable.

'What happened to the bear?' Pip asked Mopsa.

'It ate most of the apples and all the pies,' said Mopsa, 'then it went to sleep. If you ask it nicely, it will carry you back to Sunny Bay tomorrow.'

When everyone was too full to make sensible conversation, the drums started up along with some rather wild fiddle-playing. There was a good deal of noise at the furthest table: cheering followed by a loud crash. Gorbo had made a bet that he could stand on his head on a pyramid of mead jars – and lost. The Queen just sighed and shook her head.

Small Snerglets were sent home to bed. Mead pots clinked. One or two Snergs fell off their chairs. Voices swelled in song.

How marvellous to be a Snerg, in this wondrous land,
Short in height but great of heart, a grand rambunctious
*   band!*
We'll party under moon or sun,
Not stopping till the pudding's done –

'Pudding!' shouted an over-excited voice at the furthest table. Gorbo, of course.

We'll sing until we're dry with thirst,
We'll dance until our blisters burst.
No decent Snerg will go to bed,
Without first standing on his head . . .

At the word 'head', the music stopped and everybody had to jump off their chair and stand on their head. If you wobbled or fell over before the music started up again, you were out. (It is worth noting that Snergs have unusually resilient stomachs. For other people, this game can end badly after a large meal.) The Queen, as referee, stayed in her seat; it is not easy to stand on your head while wearing a very tall crown. Flora was soon out but for Pip, the circus child, turning himself upside down was a simple matter: he was used to looking at the world that way. Finally declared the winner, he was hoisted into the air and passed the length of all the tables. At the last table he looked for Gorbo but couldn't see him. *Just as well*, thought Pip, for the moon was sailing clear of the top of the oak tree. It must be past midnight and time for Gorbo to be at the ostrich house by now.

There was more dancing: the riotous sort, with a great deal of whirling and spinning and crashes and breakages. When everyone was too dizzy for any more, the cry went up for a story.

'A story! A story!' Mead pots drummed on the tabletops. 'We can't go to bed without a story? Where is she? Bring the Container of Stories!'

The Container of Stories turned out to be a very ancient Snerg, her long hair straggling out from beneath her saucer cap but her eyes still bright. She was lifted on to the table where she stood swaying, her wrinkled face turned up to the moonlight.

'Wait,' whispered Mopsa to the children. 'She's loading . . .'

The old Snerg jerked suddenly upright; she began to speak in a voice that ebbed and flowed like the waves on the beach at Sunny Bay. The story she told was the same as Gorbo had begun earlier that day – the tale of Golithos the ogre: fierce of fang and foul of breath, ferocious fiend with an indefatigable fancy for fried infants.

'She tells it better than Gorbo does,' said Mopsa, but Pip and Flora did not hear her. Weary and well-fed, lulled by the music of the old Snerg's voice, they had fallen fast asleep.

CHAPTER 16

In Pip's dream, he and Flora were riding bears. He could feel the warm fur and the rolling sway; he could smell the cinnamon. Together they rode through the high iron gates at Sunny Bay. Orphans lined up on either side of them, staring with envious eyes. At the very end of the line stood Miss Watkyns, waiting . . .

His dream-bear gave a sudden lurch and was gone. Pip's eyes flew open. Above him were leaves and birdsong, the pearly glimmer of a new morning. There was another lurch. Pip tried to sit up, floundered in mid-air, then landed with an *ummmph!* on the ground.

In front of him were the remains of last night's feast: the long wooden tables, up-ended stools and plates empty of anything but crumbs. Above his head rocked an empty hammock. Snergs are very fond of hammocks, hanging them here and there between the trees, much as other places might have park benches. As the revels broke up at last, sometime in the small, starry hours, the Queen had made sure that the sleeping children were safely tucked up for what was left of the night.

Pip blinked. Flora was standing over him, her Snerg cap jammed over her curls.

'Did you just tip me out?' he demanded.

'Tiger,' said Flora. She was holding a piece of frayed string. There wasn't a dog on the end of it. '*Tiger.*'

'What about him?' Pip yawned. 'Flora, you're *talking* again . . .'

Since their encounter with the wobsers, Flora had been silent. She knew something was happening inside her: something cold and hard was beginning to crack, like ice floes after an Arctic winter. Last night, as the Snergs roared out their songs, she had felt her voice stir in her throat, wanting to join in. She had folded her lips tight together to stop it, afraid that it would come out wrong.

Ice takes time to melt – but this was urgent. Flora had climbed out of her hammock early, the only one awake in a sleeping town. Missing Tiger, she had slipped away to Gorbo's house – and found it empty. Tiger had chewed through his string and taken himself off.

'He's *gone*.'

'Perhaps he's with Gorbo at the ostrich house.' Pip was on his feet. 'Let's go and look.'

Snergs lay everywhere, in snoring heaps, wherever sleep had overtaken them. Picking their way between them, the children had reached the end of the street and were wondering which way to turn when they saw Gorbo waving at them.

'Happy morning to you,' he said cheerfully. 'I've had a night of it! I had to fight off a squeazel – at least, I think it was a squeazel: it was long and slinky. Hard to see in the dark. It was after the ostrich chicks. Lucky for me, one of the ostriches woke up and gave it a kick that sent it flying all the way into next week. Is it time for breakfast?'

'Gorbo, have you seen Tiger?' Pip asked. 'We've lost him.'

Even before he had finished speaking, they heard it: a familiar, joyful barking. Tiger was not far away – and he had found something to chase. The sound was coming from a place where the trees grew closer together and the shadows were darker. Pip and Flora set off after it.

Gorbo hung back. 'Ah . . .' he said. 'Um . . .'

They looked over their shoulders at him. 'What?'

'We don't usually go that way.' said Gorbo.

'Why not?'

'It leads to places you don't want to go.' Gorbo reached for his lucky acorn. 'Full of things you don't want to meet . . .'

Tiger's barks were growing fainter and further off.

'You can be scared if you like,' said Flora. 'I'm not.' And she set off at a run.

Pip bit his lip, hesitating just for a moment, then he went after her.

'Heigh-ho,' said Gorbo gloomily. 'It'll be a fish spanking and the ostrich house for a month when the Queen hears about this – but what's a Snerg to do? I can't let those little half-Noodles run off by themselves, can I? Not *that* way. One wrong turn and the next thing you know, they'll have got themselves tangled up in the Twisted Trees . . .'

'It's so dark,' said Pip. 'I can hardly see.'

They had been pushing through the trees for a while, whistling and calling Tiger's name. The air was still and heavy, like it is before a storm. Above their heads the canopy had matted into a thick thatch of twigs and leaves, shutting out the sun.

'Ouch!' Pip tripped over a thick loop of tree root.

'*Ow!*' A second later, Flora had done the same thing.

'Uh-oh,' said Gorbo. He had stopped and was staring around him. 'Um . . . would you say there was anything *odd* about these trees? Would you describe them as *twisty*?'

Trees are just trees – until you bother to stop and look at them properly. Or until they start tripping you up and you get the definite feeling that they are doing it on purpose. These were not like any trees the children had seen before. Leaves grew only at the very top of their thick grey trunks; smooth bare branches looped down to touch the ground, coiling like silver serpents. The silence beat in Pip's ears. *There aren't any birds*, he realized. *Why not?*

'I do *not* think,' said Gorbo, 'that this is a sensible place to be. These are not kind trees. We should go back.'

'We can't,' Flora protested. 'Not without . . . *aaah*!'

She bit off a yell. Something had skimmed the top of her head before swooping away on leathery wings.

Pip had ducked. 'What was *that?*'

'That,' said Gorbo, 'was a bat. And not one of the little pretty, flitty sort that doesn't mean you any harm. The other sort. It really would be an excellent idea to be somewhere else.'

'Sssh – listen . . .' Flora stood with tilted head, straining to hear. A flurry of barks, then silence.

Twisting and crossing, the branches were all around them, barring their way.

'Now I know what a netted fish feels like,' puffed Gorbo, fighting his way through. 'If we get out of here, I promise I'll never go fishing again . . . well, look at that!'

In front of them was a door, cut into one of the looming trunks. It had heavy iron hinges and an ugly little face with a pointed beard for a knocker.

'Tiger's in there,' said Pip. 'I can hear him.'

The barks were muffled, as if they came from a long way underground. A small, desperate sound came from Flora.

Gorbo was inspecting the door. 'Could be goblins,' he said thoughtfully, 'though I've never heard of goblins putting a knocker on their front door. They don't care for visitors. But *somebody* went to the bother of putting it there, which means it would be rude not to use it!'

Nobody answered Gorbo's energetic knocking but the door swung slowly, creakily, open.

'Steps,' said Gorbo, peering in. 'The going-down sort. Lots of them. Smells a bit of cheese. You'd better let me go first . . . just in case.'

As Flora squeezed through the doorway after Gorbo, Pip hesitated. He might not be much good at spellings and sums but he had more than enough sense not to let a door with no handle close behind him. Looking about him, he found a round stone – heavy enough to make a useful doorstop – and rolled it carefully into place.

'Wait for me!' said Pip, starting down the steps after the others.

Not having eyes in the back of his head, he never noticed his doorstop stand up on stumpy legs and waddle away.

All it took was one puff of air, like a lost sneeze – and the door slammed shut.

CHAPTER 16½

'That,' said the lady, 'was almost too easy. The ugly little mutt has his uses. He'll chase anything through an open doorway.'

She drew her purple shawl around her, gazing into the depths of her jelly. 'The girl is on her way: Goldilocks and her two dwarves . . . or am I remembering that wrong? Now we must bring the moths a little closer to the flame. Don't you love the smell of singed wings? And that will be just the start of it. I see plumes of smoke and pillars of flame rising high, high into the sky above Sunny Bay. And then ashes . . . nothing but a pile of cold ashes. "A tragic accident",

they'll call it. "Poor little orphans. Poor Miss Watkyns."
Boohoo. My heart bleeds.'

'Poor Muzzer.' The giant at her elbow gave her a little pat.
'Don't be sad, Muzzer.'

'Idiot,' said his mother.

In which Miss Watkyns musters an Expeditionary Force and the wanderers find themselves in the Fungus Tunnels, natural habitat of the Hairy Walrus. In the Land of the Kelps, Gorbo is threatened with a parsnip and the children put their trust in cunning Fool.

CHAPTER 17

'There's a large bird in the garden.' Miss Scadging put her head around Miss Watkyns's door. 'Very large. I thought you ought to know.'

Miss Watkyns, usually so busy, had spent much of the last two days just sitting at her desk, lost in her own thoughts. *Is she even listening?* wondered Miss Scadging.

'The bird has a person with it,' she added. 'Riding it.'

This had an effect. Miss Watkyns was on her feet, looking out of the window. Down in the garden a small person, wrapped in a red riding cloak, was trying to stop an ostrich from biting the heads off a bed of dahlias.

'A Queen's Rider,' muttered Miss Watkyns. 'There's news, then; let's hope it's the right sort.'

The news was very much the *wrong* sort. When she had heard it, Miss Watkyns sat down to write a short but urgent letter to Captain Vanderdecken. Out in the garden, she found Miss Scadging feeding cucumber sandwiches to the ostrich.

'The children are not found?' asked Miss Scadging, seeing the grim look on Miss Watkyns's face.

'Found, and lost again,' said Miss Watkyns. 'I need this letter delivered to the *Flying Dutchman*. Where is Mr Gribblestone? His long legs will be the fastest.'

'He is in the schoolroom,' said Miss Scadging. 'Listening to the boys recite Latin verbs. The girls are practising their needlework. They are not trying their best today, I am afraid. The weather is so very warm.'

Miss Watkyns glanced out at the sky, a brilliant blue, and the sun-flecked sapphire sea. 'Education is an excellent thing,' she observed, 'but, like everything else, it has its time and its place. That time is not this afternoon. Take the children to the beach. Give them an outing.'

'They have just had an outing,' Miss Scadging reminded her. 'The picnic at Puffin Island.'

'Then let them take their sketchbooks and call it an art class,' said Miss Watkyns. 'Let them draw what they like: shells, gulls, sailing boats, mermaids, sea monsters . . .'

Miss Scadging looked startled. 'Sea monsters?'

Miss Watkyns sighed, passing a hand across her brow. 'There are more things on heaven and earth, Miss Scadging, than you and I are prepared to admit. Possible and impossible; real and imaginary. We choose to think there is a line separating one from the other – but that line can be rubbed out. Children come into the world knowing this. Perhaps we should stop trying to teach them that they are wrong.'

Sometime later, after one hundred and twenty-eight surprised children had been marched off to the beach, heavy boots came tramping through the orphanage gates: Captain Vanderdecken's crew marched behind him, each man with a musket over his shoulder. Miss Watkyns stood waiting to greet them, with the Queen's Rider and ostrich at her side.

Shaking the Captain's hand, she glanced a little doubt-fully at the crew. 'Are you sure your men are up to such a long journey?'

'Full of beans and raring to go, every one of them,' the Captain assured her. 'Sailors never grow too old for adven-ture. To be honest, ma'am, I think they were growing a little tired of band practice.'

'I must warn you,' said Miss Watkyns, 'that where you are going, you may see things that you find surprising . . .'

'When you have sailed the seven seas, very little surprises you,' said the Captain. 'Pirates, cannibal-infested islands, monsters with jaws that can swallow a ship from keel to rig-ging: my men have seen it all. They have the hearts of drag-ons, ma'am; nothing daunts them.' He waved a hand at the Queen's Rider. 'If this young lady and her fine bird will escort us to her people, together we shall form an Expedi-tionary Force not to be trifled with. We shall bring your lost lambs back, Miss Watkyns – word of a sailor and a gentle-man. All I ask is that you keep an eye on Mr Plankton and Mr Halibut. I thought it best to leave them on the *Dutch-man* – Mr Plankton suffers with his bunions, you know, and Mr Halibut has his stomach trouble. They are in charge of feeding the parrot and firing Dead Men Doris. The cannon must go off every day at midday *on the dot*. If I am not here to keep everything ship-shape, I fear there may be some slacking on deck.'

Promising to remind Mr Halibut and Mr Plankton of their duties, Miss Watkyns wished the Expeditionary Force good speed and good luck. With a last salute they managed an about-turn with hardly any confusion or bumping into each other, and marched away, following the ostrich's tail feathers.

Miss Watkyns sat staring at nothing. Unheeded, the goldfish darted in figures of eight. Her desk was orderly but her thoughts were not; they flapped on dark wings inside her head.

You can't lock the past away and pretend it never happened . . .

Miss Watkyns stood up. Selecting a key from the bunch hanging at her waist, she opened a locked cabinet and took out a battered old tin hat box. It had once been painted with wreaths of roses and lilies but the paint had faded long ago; the metal was dented and tarnished, with a crust of something that looked very like barnacles. Squaring her shoulders, Miss Watkyns drew a deep breath and lifted the lid. There was not much inside. A sheet of paper folded very small, a piece of knotted string, a scattering of little shells and one half of a silver heart on a string of coral beads. With a hand that was not quite steady, she smoothed out the paper. The writing was in a childish hand, splattered with ink blots. Miss Watkyns's lips moved as she read.

> When the moon shines bright on the Only Yew,
> When white owls hoot and black cats mew,
> When the dog fox barks and bats flit,
> Bricks will blacken, flames will spit.
> Ashes to ashes, dust to dust,
> House of misery: end it must.

Miss Watkyns sighed. 'It was a long time ago,' she murmured, 'and we were very young – which excuses the poetry, if nothing else.' Picking up the coral necklace she let the beads drop into her palm, her eyes on the little broken heart. 'Yes, this was a place of misery once; we promised that we would see it fall – but there is more than one way to keep a promise. Mr Bunphatt is gone, and it is different now. The children here do not suffer as we did. I do my best to keep them safe. Stay away, Malicia. Stay away from Pip and Flora . . .'

CHAPTER 18

'It could be worse,' said Gorbo. 'At least we can see where we're going . . .'

The steps leading down inside the hollow tree were narrow, but the toadstools growing from the damp walls gave out a faint green glow.

The door that had slammed behind Pip was shut fast; it would not budge.

'No use moping,' said Gorbo. 'There's no going backwards and there's no going sideways, so we'll have to go forwards.'

Just as it began to seem that the steps would go on for

ever, down and down into the earth's core, at last the travellers found themselves with their feet on flat ground. The walls opened out into a wide cavern. Lit by the luminous walls, a forest of monstrous mushrooms rose up all around them. And there, in front of them, cheerfully cocking his leg on a mushroom stalk . . . was Tiger.

He bounced up to them, tail wagging, not looking at all sorry for the trouble he had caused.

'If it wasn't for you,' Gorbo told him, 'we'd all be digesting a good breakfast by now. Now here we are on the wrong side of the Twisted Trees, who knows how far underground, and nothing to eat but fungus.'

Standing underneath a mushroom, he looked up at the pale gills spreading out above his head like an umbrella.

'Complicated things, mushrooms,' said Gorbo thoughtfully. 'Some you can eat, some you can't – unless you want to be ill, or dead, or both. My Great Uncle Lumpus was a toadstool farmer. What was it he used to say?

Red spots on white, sick all night,
White spots on red, that's all right.
I think that was it. Unless it was:

White spots on red, dead in bed,

Red spots on white, nice with bread.

If I could only remember which . . .'

'It wouldn't help much,' said Pip. 'These don't have any spots. But *something's* been eating them.' A number of the mushroom caps had large half-moon shaped pieces bitten out of them. 'Something with a big mouth. Look at the teeth marks.'

'Well, if *something* can eat them, so can we,' decided Gorbo. 'It's long past breakfast time and if we're going to be lost underground, we might as well do it with a full stomach.' Reaching up on tiptoe, he broke a piece off the mushroom cap, sniffed it carefully, then put it in his mouth and chewed. He went on chewing for quite a long time. 'Might taste better cooked,' he said hopefully. 'It's a good thing I happen to have my toasting fork and some wild garlic.' Shrugging his string bag off his shoulder, he looked at the dried stalks littering the ground. 'Plenty of fuel. What we need now is a neat little fire.'

CHAPTER 18½

'They're doing it wrong, Muzzer.' The giant peered into the jelly, over the woman's shoulder. 'If they eat the mushrooms, they will have to stay down there for ever.'

The woman pushed the skull bowl away from her, making the jelly wobble. 'Must Snergs always be thinking of their stomachs?' Eyes flashing, she stamped her foot in its violet stocking. 'I have waited all these years; I have laid my plans with care. I won't have them spoilt by that little hog Gorbo's greed. I won't! Where is Gubbins? He was supposed to lead them to me, not leave them to stuff themselves with enchanted fungus.'

'Bruzzer Gubbins is naughty – he doesn't do as he's told,' said the ogre. 'Not like me, Muzzer. Perhaps Gubbins has eaten the mushrooms too, and won't ever come back . . . I wouldn't do that, Muzzer. I'm your good little boy. Would you miss me, if I had to stay in the Mushroom Halls for ever and ever?'

'Of course I'd miss you,' said his mother. 'In the same way I'd miss fleabites and earwax and a stone in my shoe . . .'

CHAPTER 19

The smell of toasted garlic mushroom wafting through the fungus tunnels might have had something to do with what happened next – or maybe it was chance. Who knows?

'Hot,' warned Gorbo, handing Flora a slice of mushroom.

It was juicy, crisped golden by the fire, and Flora was hungry. She was blowing on it, about to take her first bite, when she suddenly froze.

They had all heard it. *Fffulump . . . fffulump . . . fffulump . . .* coming from one of the many tunnels leading off from the cavern. It sounded like someone dragging a heavy sack – and it was coming closer.

'What *is* it?' whispered Pip.

Gorbo was on his feet, toasting fork at the ready.

'Fear not,' he declared. 'Whatever it is, if we don't like the look of it, I'll *prong* it.'

Tiger was bristling and growling. Flora dropped her mushroom and grabbed hold of him, just in time.

The creature that came flopping out of the tunnel looked very like a walrus – supposing walruses had golden-blonde fur and the sort of pocket kangaroos keep their babies in. Shuffling on hairy flippers, it reached up to tear at the mushroom caps with its tusks, bundling what it didn't eat into its pocket and rumbling with a deep, satisfied purr.

Tiger wriggled in Flora's arms, yapping. The purring stopped. The creature's bulging eyes swivelled. Gorbo took a step forward, placing himself between it and the children. The walrus puffed its cheeks, blowing out its moustache.

'Very fine,' said Gorbo. 'Two can play at that.' And he puffed out his own cheeks, making his face rounder than ever.

The walrus stared and thumped its tail.

Gorbo stamped his boots.

Who knows what might have happened next if, at that moment, another walrus had not come *fffulump*ing out of one of the other tunnels. It was helping itself to the nearest mushroom when it spotted the first walrus. Eyes rolling, the two beasts shuffled around to face each other, rumbling and cheek-puffing and thumping the ground. Rearing up, they tossed their heads, showing off their tusks, then crashed into each other, trying to push each other backwards.

'It looks to me,' said Gorbo disapprovingly, 'as if they have never learnt to share. All that pushing and shoving when there are enough mushrooms here to feed a whole huddle of walruses!'

'They'll hurt each other,' worried Pip.

'Fluster and bluster, if you ask me,' said Gorbo. 'But as they do seem to be the excitable type, it might be a good moment to leave. I don't like walking away from an uneaten breakfast, but those tusks look quite sharp.'

As Pip and Flora had been thinking rather the same thing, they stamped out the fire and crept as quietly as possible towards the mouth of the nearest tunnel.

'Seeing as we don't know where any of them go, we may

as well take this one,' said Gorbo. 'Better stick close together, in case of any more surprises.'

They had gone some way, lit by the green glow of toadstools, when they heard *fffulump, fffulump* coming fast behind them. There was no time to do anything but press themselves flat against the tunnel walls and hope for the best. Flip-flopping around a bend in the tunnel, a walrus galumphed into sight. It had seen them. It halted, rolling wild eyes in the fungus-light, then covered its whiskery face with its flippers. Everybody held their breath.

Even a walrus can only hold its breath for so long. Peeping out between its flippers, finding Gorbo and the children still there, it uttered a roaring sob and fled past them, scattering bits of mushroom as it went.

'I suppose that was the loser,' guessed Pip.

'Over-sensitive,' said Gorbo sadly, shaking his head.

The tunnel led them on, until they found themselves standing at a fork.

'Which way?' wondered Pip.

'You should always turn left on Tuesdays,' said Gorbo.

'Everyone knows that.'

'I don't think it's Tuesday . . .' said Pip.

'You shouldn't walk backwards under a full moon,' offered Gorbo instead. 'My grandmother always said so. She had a lot of useful sayings. It's bad luck to sneeze on Midsummer's Eve. And if you ever find a caterpillar in your left ear you should put it on a cabbage leaf and sing "Happy Birthday" to it.'

'Right . . .' said Pip doubtfully.

'Or possibly left,' said Gorbo.

Flora ran out of patience. 'I know what to do.'

Hiding behind her hair, she had never joined in with the other girls' games at Sunny Bay but she had listened and learnt their rhymes.

'Eeny meeny macaraca
Rare rye dominacka
Chickalacka lollipoppa
Om pom push!'

Flora's pointing finger moved from right to left, then stopped. 'That way,' she said.

CHAPTER 19½

'What magic words are these?' The woman sat hunched over her jelly. 'The child knows dark arts already . . . I knew she was the one. I saw the anger in her, all bottled up. I shall let it out. She will be my pupil. When I have bent her to my will, I shall teach her everything I know.'

'She looks so sweet and tender . . . and buttery,' sighed the giant. 'She would be nicer stuffed with sage and onion than with clever learnings. Couldn't you teach me instead?'

'You? If you learn how to wipe your own nose, it will be

a miracle. Move, you great slab of rock.' She jabbed at him with a sharp elbow. 'Don't breathe on the jelly! You're fogging it. And be quiet, I want to hear . . .'

CHAPTER 19 ¾

'*Ip dip, sky blue
Who's it? Not you!*'

They had stopped at yet another fork. Flora was running out of rhymes. They were all getting tired of tunnels and toadstools.

'If you ask me,' said Pip, 'we're going around in circles.'

Flora gave him a look. 'Go on, then – *you* find the way out.' The rhymes had loosened her voice. She might have said more but she was interrupted by Tiger who suddenly squeezed past her legs and went rocketing off down the left-hand tunnel, leaving his barks echoing behind him.

'Tiger!' exclaimed Flora. 'Not *again*!'

'Flibbertigibbet animal,' grumbled Gorbo. 'What's he found to chase this time?'

He didn't say so – it was hard to be sure in the dim, green light – but Pip thought he had seen something: a dark shadow slinking around a bend in the tunnel.

They called Tiger's name as they went, listening for an answering bark. At last they caught up with him, sitting scratching a flea-bothered ear at the bottom of a flight of stone steps.

'Steps again,' said Pip. 'Do you suppose . . . ?'

'Yes, I do,' said Gorbo. 'What comes down, must go up. That dog deserves a pie, all to himself. He's found the way out!'

They climbed until their legs hurt, their pace slowing as the steps grew narrower and steeper. Gorbo led the way, toasting fork in hand, just in case. At last they reached the top. Cut into the rock in front of them was the outline of a door.

'Stand back,' ordered Gorbo. Handing Flora the toasting fork, he pulled his cap down over his ears and retreated down a few steps. 'Best to get a run-up,' he explained, then lowered his head like a small, determined bull . . . and charged.

The door swung open without even a creak, and Gorbo flew straight through.

CHAPTER 20

Daylight seemed very bright after the green glow of the fungus tunnels. Gorbo sat on a tuft of grass with his eyes crossed.

'Is anyone else seeing stars?' he wondered. 'The flying-about sort? Quite pretty . . .'

'I think it's just you,' said Pip. 'You landed on your head. Where are we?'

They were standing on top of a hill. The ground around them was dry and stony, dotted with clumps of scrubby grass and stunted thorn trees. In the valley below, rushing water frothed over boulders. On the other side of the river, they could see the writhing shadows of the Twisted Trees and beyond them, the green and cheerful places they had left behind.

'That's the thing about rivers,' sighed Gorbo. 'Things always look better on the other side. In this case, because they are. I've an unpleasant feeling we've come out in Kelp country. Not a good thing. They're not nice: babies boiled with rice and all that . . . We should go back.'

'We can't,' said Flora, with a shiver. 'The door's gone.' She was right. The slab of rock behind them, through which Gorbo had just burst, was now smooth and solid, without any trace of an opening.

'A person can have enough of magic doors,' said Gorbo crossly, rubbing his sore head. 'It makes you want to see your own front door – one that knows its place and doesn't spring nasty surprises on you. If I ever get home, I'll give mine a new coat of paint. I've been taking it for granted all these years, in and out without even a please or thank you.'

Pip looked out across the plain below them, flat and dusty. In the middle of it squatted a hill shaped like a pudding bowl, its summit crowned with a high wall and battlements.

'There's a town over there.' He pointed. 'Is that where the Kelps live?'

Gorbo nodded. 'Banrive, they call it. Not very welcoming, is it? Doesn't exactly shout "Come to tea; we'd love to see you and there's plenty of pie". I don't know who they're trying to keep out with those walls. Golithos used to make a nuisance of himself, both sides of the river, but that was a long time ago. They say he's quite a different fellow now.'

'Golithos?' Pip frowned. 'The ogre? "Foul of breath and fierce of fang?" But that was just a story - wasn't it?'

Gorbo looked surprised. 'I don't know what they taught you in that orphanage,' he said severely, 'but it seems to me that they put some fuzzy-witted notions in your head. There's no such thing as *just* a story. Golithos is as real as you and I, but not the ogre he used to be – quite harmless now from what I hear. I'm not saying he *wanted* to be re-formed – he wasn't given much choice in the matter. I don't know about his breath, but you don't have to worry about his fangs these days – not unless you're a cabbage.'

As they stood gazing out across the plain, a gate opened in those unwelcoming city walls. Tiny in the distance, little figures streamed out of it. Shading his eyes, Gorbo gave a gasp.

'Kelps! It's even worse than I feared . . . they've got *four legs*!'

Flora squinted into the distance. 'They're riding horses, Gorbo.' She wasn't used to hearing her thoughts coming out as words. They still felt strange in her mouth; she had to cough, to clear her throat.

'And they're wearing armour,' said Pip, catching the glint of sunlight on metal.

'That's just like them.' Gorbo sniffed, recovering himself. 'What sensible person dresses up like a tin can on a sunny day? Off to do some biting and screaming and kicking, I suppose! It's time we got out of here – the question is *how*. We can't get back *under* the river, and it would be a very long journey to go *around* the river. We could try going *through* the river, but I'm not at all sure that's a sensible plan. It looks to me like exactly the sort of river a crocopotamus would choose to live in.'

'Crocopotamus.' Flora liked that word. She said it again. 'Crocopotamus.'

Pip stared down at the river. 'A what-a-potamus?'

'Oh, you know the sort of thing,' said Gorbo. 'Tail one end, scales in the middle and a mouth at the other end, big enough to swallow you whole. They hang about just under the water, pretending they're not there. By the time you know they *are* there, you're generally looking at the inside of their stomach.'

'I think,' said Pip, 'that I'd rather not meet one.'

'In that case,' said Gorbo, 'all that's left is to go *over* the river. What we need is a bridge!'

CHAPTER 20½

'How many times have I told you about using a handkerchief when you sneeze? Now look what you've done!' The woman bent over her skull bowl, picking out chips of gravel.

'I can't help it, Muzzer.' The giant wiped his nose on the back of his hand. 'I can't help all the little stones flying out of my snotrils when I aaaa-shnoo . . .'

'Just like your rock troll of a father,' snapped the woman. 'Nothing but rubble and stone dust where your brains should be. Must you spray it all into my jelly? I shall have to melt it down and strain it through a stocking, thanks to you having a snout like an erupting volcano.' She stared into the skull through narrowed eyes; it showed her nothing but pock-marked jelly. 'We've lost them. And just as that stupid Snerg is about to lead them to the bridge.'

'They won't get across, Muzzer,' the giant comforted her. 'Not across the Troll Bridge.'

'No, they won't,' she agreed. 'And why is that, my granite-witted genius?'

'Because the Troll will munch and crunch them up,' said her son, pleased at knowing the answer. Something flickered, among the pebbles of his brain. 'But, Muzzer . . . the juicy girl . . . we don't want the Troll to eat her.'

The woman gave a crack of sarcastic laughter. 'Quite right, my igneous imbecile: we don't. After the trouble I've been to, I won't let that girl end up as a troll's dinner. Go after them. The Troll may have the Snerg, with my compliments, and the boy too – but bring me that girl.'

CHAPTER 21

The travellers set off downhill, keeping the river to one side of them and the distant battlements of Banrive to the other. Gorbo led the way, holding his bow: 'Just in case.'

Tiger trotted at Flora's heels, kept to heel by means of a length of string.

They were walking beneath a cluster of spindly pine trees when Gorbo came to a sudden halt.

'Did you hear that? I thought I heard . . . jingling.'

'Got you, Snerg!' said a voice.

Something brightly coloured dropped out of the branches above his head and Gorbo went down backwards with a *wmphhh!*

The voice belonged to a sharp-faced young man, all in scarlet and yellow, with bells on the pointed toes of his shoes and on the horns of his hood. He sat astride the winded Gorbo, pressing something sharp against his ribs.

'Yield, scurril Snerg!' ordered the young man. 'Or I shall smite you!'

'Get off!' said Flora. 'You're squashing him.'

Pip looked at the gaudy red and yellow costume and the small stringed instrument slung from the man's shoulder. 'Are you from a circus?'

'My life's work is to ease the sorrows of the world,' said the young man grandly, 'with my merry songs and jolly jests. At your service, sire – Baldry, King Kul's Fool at the Kelp Court.' He swept a low bow over Gorbo's chest.

'You're not easing my sorrows,' objected Gorbo. 'I can't breathe, and your bells are going up my nose.'

'We must bind this Snerg!' declared the jester. 'Their bite is poisonous, you know. It is a lucky thing that I happened to be sitting in this tree, with nothing better to do than save you poor innocent children from being lured to his lair.'

'You don't know what you're talking about,' said Flora.

'Step away, fair damsel.' The jester lifted his weapon. 'Do not be alarmed. If it puts up a fight, I shall run it through with my—'

'Parsnip,' said Pip. 'Anyone can see that's a parsnip. And Gorbo is our friend. Leave him alone, or we'll set our dog on you.'

'Not much of a dog.' The jester looked critically at Tiger. 'More of a pompom. Does anyone have any rope about them?'

'I have some string,' offered Gorbo.

'Don't give it to him, Gorbo,' said Flora crossly. 'He wants to tie you up.'

'We won't let him,' added Pip.

'Alas, I see the Snerg has tricked you both most thoroughly,' mourned the jester. 'Never fear, Baldry is here. Prepare to meet your fate, cannibal dumpling.'

This was too much for Gorbo. With a heave, he tipped the jester sideways and wriggled free. 'Who are you calling a cannibal dumpling?' he demanded. 'Everyone knows it is the Kelps who eat children.'

'Hold your tongue, snivelling Snerg!' retorted Baldry. 'And hand over your string. I shall truss you up, like a spider with a fly, and deliver you to King Kul. The reward for capturing strangers – especially Snergs – is seventeen pieces of silver. Poor Baldry is out of favour with the King just now . . .'

'Why?' asked Pip.

Baldry sniffed. 'Artists such as myself are so often misunderstood. The King took offence at a fine jest, involving a quantity of butter and the palace steps – and, as it turned out, some bruising of royal behinds. But if I bring him a Snerg, he will forgive his Baldry. And even if he doesn't, he'll still owe me seventeen pieces of silver.'

He made a grab for Gorbo but found himself facing Pip and Flora. They stood shoulder to shoulder – Pip with his fists up, Flora with hands on hips.

'Avaunt, puny infants!' cried the jester, lunging at them with his parsnip. 'Let me at that Snerg – *ow*!'

Tiger, pulling on his string, had snapped at the tinkling bells on Baldry's feet. Jaws closing around the upturned toe of a scarlet shoe, he shook it like a rat.

'Call off your pompom!' demanded the jester, hopping on one foot.

'I'm giving you two options, Mr Baldry.' Gorbo appeared between the children with his bowstring drawn back. 'Option one: I shoot you. Snerg arrows are dipped in a concoction made of the juice of the forget-me-now flower and the dribble of the deliriously dreaming dormouse. You will fall instantly asleep – but there is a definite risk that by the time you wake up, we will have thrown you in the river for the crocopotami to play with.'

Baldry looked at Gorbo's arrow, which was pointing directly at his stomach. 'What's option two?' he asked sulkily.

'Guide us to the nearest bridge,' said Gorbo. 'We arrived here by mistake and we want to go home again, across the river and back to the Land of the Snergs.'

Baldry raised his eyebrows. 'There's only one bridge that I know of – the Troll Bridge. But you can't cross it.'

'Why not?' demanded Gorbo.

'Why do you think, thickhead?' sneered Baldry. 'The clue's in the name. There's a troll living under it. Big hairy pudding of a beast, with a nose like the worst kind of sausage. She doesn't stir herself much but if she hears you three *trip-trapping* over her bridge, she'll be out in a flash and that'll be the end of at least one of you. Probably her,' he added, nodding at Flora. 'A hungry troll would find her toothsome, I should think – no, don't shoot!'

Gorbo had raised his bow. The jester sank to his knees, as well as he could with a puppy still attached to his shoe. 'Wait,' he begged. 'Let's not be too hasty. I can be useful to you. Call off your dog, put down your bow and I'll tell you how.'

Gorbo lowered his bow, still looking suspicious, while Flora prised a growling Tiger off the jester's foot.

'Kelps do not like strangers.' Baldry inspected the damage to his shoe. 'They are to be arrested on sight and taken straight to King Kul: that is the law. If you go trotting about in the open, you'll be captured in no time. You'll be dragged off to Banrive and the King will have your heads off, quick as winking, and planted on spikes.'

'Does he . . . does he plant a lot of heads?' asked Pip, with an unpleasant sinking feeling in his insides.

'It's absolutely his favourite thing,' said Baldry airily. 'He keeps a Grand High Executioner, a High Executioner and a Medium-Height Executioner all working a six-day week. He is the fiercest and cruellest tyrant that ever wore a crown. But do not despair – I know a person who may be able to help you. She has a hovel not far from here, on the edge of the Distressful Swamp.'

'Don't like the sound of it,' decided Gorbo, raising his bow again.

'Hear me out,' begged Baldry. 'The old woman's harmless. Keeps herself to herself, lives alone with a bunch of cats. People take their problems to her: anything from a sick cow to a broken heart. I've heard that she has been seen on the other side of the river. She must know a way across.'

'How do we know *she* won't sell us for seventeen pieces of silver?' Gorbo wanted to know.

The bells on Baldry's head jingled as he shook his head. 'Not her. She won't risk showing her face in Banrive. It is against the law to practise magic in these lands – on pain of being slowly lowered into a pit of sabre-toothed centipedes.'

'Magic?' Gorbo frowned. 'You mean she's a witch?'

'I told you,' said Baldry, 'just charms and potions – but

that's enough for King Kul. One bad experience, a long time ago, and now he's terrified of any kind of magic. That's why she lives out of sight, near the swamp. There are good witches as well as bad, you know.'

'True,' agreed Gorbo. 'The problem is telling which witch is which.'

Baldry shrugged. 'She's your only hope. You can trust me. Word of a jester.'

So it was that Gorbo and the children turned their back on the river – across which lay friends and safety and the promise of home – and never stopped to ask themselves: is it wise to trust a clever Fool?

CHAPTER 22

Some houses look pleased to see you. Others don't. Widow Meldrum's cottage crouched low, frowning under the thatch that straggled over its windows like a badly cut fringe. Buddleia stalks sprayed out of the roof and black bryony grew over the arched doorway, which had the unfriendly look of a downturned mouth. A signpost was planted in front of it, its wooden fingers pointing in opposite directions. Gorbo ducked his head between his legs, puzzling over the scratched letters.

'*SESRUC*,' he read. 'Or *SGNISSELB*. Very helpful, I don't think.'

'*CURSES.*' Flora was looking at them the right way up. 'Or *BLESSINGS.*' She peered at a sheet of paper nailed between them. '*M. Meldrum, Musical Instruction in the Bladder Pipe, Beginner to Advanced, Enquire Within.*'

'Curses?' Gorbo looked accusingly at Baldry. 'I thought you said she was a good witch.'

Baldry shrugged. 'The old dear has to earn her bread somehow – and Kelps are very fond of quarrelling with each other. Why shouldn't she sell a few curses, if that's what people want?'

'We don't want one,' said Gorbo firmly. 'We'll go the Blessings way.'

Rounding the corner of the cottage, they came to a gate in a thick and thorny hedge. Pushing it open, they stepped through into a patch of tall stinging nettles and spiked thistles. A dying apple tree raised its bare branches to the sky. As they picked their way between nettle and thistle towards the rickety porch, something shot out from behind the apple tree. Hurtling towards them with the speed of one of Captain Vanderdecken's cannon balls, it lowered its horned head and caught Gorbo in the seat of his breeches, tossing him into the air. Gorbo's shout of surprise was cut off, turning to bubbles as he landed, headfirst, in a barrel of rainwater.

'Gorbo!' Looking anxiously at his kicking legs, the children rushed to help but the big black goat had swung around. Yellow-eyed, it raked the ground with one cloven hoof. Nimble Baldry was already halfway up the apple tree.

The cottage door creaked open. A bundle of old rags stood there, bent with age, holding a cooking pot and a picked bone.

'Mr Horniman, come for your dinner.' Her voice was as frail as the rest of her, cracked and quavering. She banged the bone against the metal pan and the goat turned and trotted up to her, meek as a lamb. From beneath the hood of her tattered gown, she considered her visitors.

'You're an odd lot,' she commented, watching Pip and Flora turn a dripping Gorbo the right way up. 'Must you drown your fleas in my water barrel, Mr Snerg?'

'You have an odd notion of blessings,' declared Gorbo when he had finished spluttering.

The old woman smiled. 'Few come this far through the

woods just to ask for a blessing. Most of my visitors come wanting curses.'

'Not us,' said Gorbo. 'We don't want to cause any trouble. All we're looking for is a nice happy ending.'

The woman shook her head. 'I can't help you with that. Happy endings are not for sale. You must make your own. Who is that, roosting like a parrot in my apple tree?'

With a jingle of bells, Baldry dropped to the ground and turned a tinkling cartwheel. 'Baldry, Court Jester, Purveyor of Hilarity by Royal Appointment at your service, ma'am. I bring you this fine fellow of a Snerg and these innocent children, all of them lost and lonely and needing your help to get them across the river and back where they belong.'

'People are always expecting favours to come free,' sighed the old woman. 'I have Mr Horniman and half a dozen or more little kitty-cats to feed – and barely a crust for my own mouth. See, I have to stitch my clothes out of rat skins.' She stuck out a foot. Rat tails trailed from the heels of her slippers. Flora took a step backwards. 'If you want my help . . . what's it worth?'

There was a silence.

'This.' Digging around in his pocket, Gorbo pulled out the coin Miss Watkyns had given him. 'It has a king's head on it. And when Miss Watkyns hears that you helped to rescue these children and get them home to Sunny Bay, she will give you more; she is a most wise and generous lady.'

'I have heard of this admirable Miss Watkyns . . .' Slipping the coin into her pocket, the old woman looked at the children. 'So, you two want to go back to Sunny Bay, do you? Why?'

The children thought of the gulls and the glint of the sea, hot buttered toast and hot chocolate and extra custard on Sundays. They remembered the sound of the bees buzzing in the lavender bushes and Miss Scadging's voice reading them stories on rainy afternoons. Even lessons with Mr Gribblestone didn't seem quite so tiresome . . . A wave of homesickness rippled through them.

'It's where we belong,' said Pip. 'It's . . .'

'. . . home,' said Flora.

The goat had finished his meal. He butted the old woman's legs, hoping for more. Pushing him away, she picked up the empty pan and turned to go back indoors.

'Well?' She looked over her shoulder at her visitors. 'What are you waiting for? You had better come in.'

In which Gorbo braves the dangers of the Distressful Swamp and Wilmus risks getting eaten by a crocopotamus. Flora learns a lesson about accepting gingerbread from strangers, something surprising happens to Baldry and King Kul's Kelps come galloping.

CHAPTER 23

Widow Meldrum's little kitty-cats turned out to be huge creatures, black as night, with elongated legs and emerald eyes.

'Rathbones, Pyewacket, Grimalkin, Hodge, Vinegar Tom, Sister Gutspill and . . . one missing, as usual,' said the old woman.

'Oh, Tiger, *no!*' Flora was struggling to hold on to him. Tiger was a puppy not much bothered by ideas of right and wrong, but he had one rule: if it moves, chase it – and the one thing that needed chasing more than any other was a cat. The sight of six at once, all staring at him with a challenge in their green eyes, was too much.

He broke free, leaping from Flora's arms, and Widow Meldrum's kitchen exploded into a whirlwind of bristling, flying fur. Claws swiped, backs arched, tails lashed. Baldry hopped up on to a chair, Gorbo covered his ears against the barking and hissing and caterwauling, while Flora and Pip tried desperately to catch hold of the troublemaker who had started it all.

Tiger, as the saying goes, had bitten off more than he could chew. It might have ended badly for him, had Widow Meldrum not intervened. Kicking cats out of the way, she reached into the rumpus and picked him up by the scruff of the neck. He was trembling, his nose scratched and one ear torn. Flora reached out for him, but the widow shook her head.

'He'll be safer up here.'

Widow Meldrum had a number of things hanging from her kitchen ceiling: strings of onions, bleached bird skulls, hollowed turnips carved into odd little faces – and two wicker cages. In one of them squatted a large toad with mournful golden eyes.

'Company for Mr B,' said the widow, putting Tiger into the second cage and shutting the door on him.

Flora bit her lip, hearing Tiger's whimper, but the cats were circling below him – fur bristling, eyes glaring – so she didn't argue.

Gorbo had uncovered his ears and was snuffing the air. 'I don't know what it is,' he remarked, 'but *something* is music to my nose.'

They were all sniffing now. Whatever it was, it smelt a little like cinnamon bear and reminded the travellers that they hadn't eaten since last night's feast.

Widow Meldrum smiled. 'You can look,' she said, whisking the muslin cloth off something on the kitchen table. 'But you mustn't nibble.'

It was a gingerbread house: a grand creation with three storeys, tall chimneys and iced gables. It made Flora think of the dolls' house in her lonely nursery. It reminded Pip of something else, but he wasn't sure what. The little marzipan faces at the shuttered windows troubled him.

Climbing down from his chair, Baldry reached out a hand; the widow slapped it away.

'I said *no nibbling*. There's work to be done, if you want to get across the Troll Bridge. Trolls are easy to deal with if you know how . . . and that's through their stomachs. We'll leave her a gift – a little something spiced with poppy and mandragora. She'll gobble it down and soon be too woozy to notice a small traveller, or three, slip past her.'

'An excellent plan,' approved Gorbo.

'It would be,' agreed the widow, who had opened a cupboard and was inspecting the shelves. 'Except that . . . oh, dear . . . I seem to have run out of mandrake root. Somebody will have to pick me some more.' She pointed at Gorbo. '*You.*'

'Me?' Gorbo scratched his woolly head. 'But where am I to find them?'

'In the Distressful Swamp,' said Widow Meldrum. 'No need to look so worried, scaredy-cat. It's a delightful place – just watch out for the snotril worms and the sabre-toothed centipedes and the vampire butterflies. And there's an especially unpleasant sort of mud-squeazel that will try to wrap itself around your ankle and drag you down. And if any bog-goblins come and chatter at you don't, whatever you do, look them in the eye. You will be perfectly safe – as long as you don't tread on a howling slug. They make enough noise to wake the things you *really* don't want to meet. You must go now, while there is still light enough to find them by, but you can't pick them until the moonlight shines on them. It is very important to remember that – or the spell won't work.'

'Will I have to wait long?' Gorbo was looking unhappy. 'In the dark? By myself?'

'We'll come with you, Gorbo,' said Pip, very much not wanting to. He looked at Flora.

She swallowed and nodded. 'What's a snotril worm?'

'They climb up your nose and suck your brains, until there is nothing left. Although as I have no brains to start with,' said Gorbo hopefully, 'it might not be so very bad.'

'The children will stay with me,' said Widow Meldrum. 'What sort of a person would send two innocent children out into a swamp, just as night was falling? Whatever would Miss Watkyns say?'

That was easy. 'She'd say it was against the rules,' said Pip. Only two days ago that would have been enough to make him *want* to squelch about in a swamp by moonlight, but a good deal had happened in those two days. Pip had wanted adventure. He was beginning to realize that while the right sort of adventure is a fine and exhilarating thing, the wrong sort makes you wish you'd stayed at home. Vampire butterflies and howling slugs sounded very much like the wrong sort of adventure.

'Baldry could go,' suggested Flora.

'Into a swamp? In these shoes?' Baldry did a little skip, toes tinkling. 'No, thank you.'

'A fuss about nothing,' scolded Widow Meldrum, handing Gorbo a sack and a lantern. 'You can't miss the way – downhill until your feet get wet – and you'll know a mandrake when you hear one. They squeal when you pull them up. I shall need at least a dozen fat ones. No use coming back without them, not if you want to get home. You may take a drop of my elderberry cordial to keep the damp out of your bones, and a piece of gingerbread to give you strength; mandrakes can be stubborn.' Breaking one of the chimneys off the gingerbread house, she gave it to Gorbo.

'You will take care of the children, won't you?' he asked anxiously. 'While I am gone?'

'As if they were my very own,' said Widow Meldrum.

As she locked the door behind Gorbo, Pip and Flora felt a pang of loss and loneliness. A draught of air had set all the little turnip heads swinging. They looked as if they were laughing, and not at all in a nice way.

'Poor weary children, you must get some sleep,' said Widow Meldrum. 'There is a cosy little bedroom upstairs where you may be snug.'

'We're not tired,' said Pip, smothering a yawn. 'We'd rather wait for Gorbo.'

'He won't be back for hours,' said the old woman, 'and you'll have an early start tomorrow, with far to travel. Didn't I promise to look after you? And so I shall – as if I were your own mother.'

Flora thought of her mother, who had cared so much more about table manners and going to parties than she had about her daughter. Pip thought of Belle the Bareback Bombshell, who had run away and left him alone with his father. Neither of them put much trust in mothers.

'If you are good children and go quietly up to bed, you may have a treat,' coaxed the old woman. 'You may have a piece of my gingerbread. Come, help yourselves. Not you,' she snapped at Baldry, who was holding out his hand. 'You may sleep over there, in that box.'

'It's full of cats,' objected Baldry.

The widow shrugged. 'You can sleep standing up then. Or outside with Mr Horniman, if you prefer.'

Flora had broken a chunk off the gingerbread roof. 'Mmm,' she said, with her mouth full, and broke off a bit more.

The widow smiled. 'Now you,' she said to Pip, handing him a piece.

Pip nibbled it, frowning. As it melted on his tongue, he suddenly knew what was wrong with that gingerbread house. 'It's Sunny Bay,' he said. 'It's the orphanage.' As he looked at the little marzipan faces with their round, open mouths, he felt a cold prickling at the back of his neck. 'And there are all the children. We're all . . . screaming.'

At that moment a shadow darkened the window. Tiger barked, setting his cage swinging from the ceiling. A black shape leapt through the open casement: a cat with one eye, ears tattered and scarred and a kink at the end of his tail.

'Not another one!' complained Baldry. 'Ugly brute, isn't he?'

Widow Meldrum glanced over her shoulder. 'Oh, him,' she said. 'Late, as usual. That's Gubbins.'

Gubbins! Flora froze, a morsel of gingerbread halfway to her lips. Pip's prickle turned into a cold rush of fear. He swung towards the door, but the widow had pocketed the key. Something leaning against the wall caught his eye . . . a purple umbrella. And lying next to it, looking small and lonely all by itself, was Flora's missing slinker.

CHAPTER 24

'He likes *you*,' said Widow Meldrum.

Gubbins was winding around Flora's legs. Flora stood like a statue, only her throat moving as she swallowed. Pip could see the fear in her eyes. The thud of his own heart was making him feel sick.

'It's time little children were in bed, sweetly snoring. And little dogs.' Lifting Tiger's cage from its hook, the woman started up the crooked stairs. There was no chance of escape. There was nothing to do but follow.

'You'll be snug as bugs in here.' Pushing the children in front of her, Widow Meldrum stood in the attic doorway.

'Don't mind the washing.'

Pip and Flora raised their eyes to the line of brightly coloured underwear hanging from a beam above their heads. Stockings in shades of lilac, mauve, violet, magenta, aubergine and plum were held in place by a row of bats, wings wrapped around hairy bodies as they dangled, dreaming their upside-down dreams.

'Make yourselves at home.' Widow Meldrum pointed at a narrow straw-stuffed mattress. Nailed to the wall above it was something black and shrivelled. 'Home is where the heart is.' Her laugh was unpleasant. 'Sleep well. No need to worry about anything at all – Mother Meldrum will take care of everything. Mother knows best . . .'

She turned to go with her cats at her heels, chasing her rat-tail slippers. Only one stayed behind. Now that Gubbins had finally found Flora, he seemed reluctant to leave her side. Ignoring Tiger's frenzied objections, he curled up on a rickety chair, watching her with his one green eye.

Pip and Flora sat huddled on the mattress.

'She doesn't *look* like the lady in the car,' said Pip.

'We couldn't see her properly under that hat.' Flora was

feeding gingerbread to Tiger through the bars of his cage, to quieten him. She did not dare let him out with Gubbins there. 'Pip, what's she going to do to us?'

'I don't know . . .'

The children sat in scared, unhappy silence, both wondering the same thing. Had they, by mistake, got into the sort of adventure that ends the worst possible way – the sort where you never, ever find your way home?

'I wish she hadn't sent Gorbo away,' said Flora.

Pip heard the quiver in her voice. 'We'll get out of here and go and look for him. Then we'll find the bridge and—'

'What about the Troll?' Flora reminded him. 'And the crocopotamus?'

Pip stood up and went to look out of the window. He had to stand on tiptoe. It was small and high, with no glass in it; the shutters hung, crooked and broken, and the overhanging thatch did not let in much light. They might be able to squeeze out of it, just, but there was a long drop down to the ground. A rustling behind him made him turn. Dusk was falling; the bats were beginning to stir. As they unfurled like hairy blossoms, scratching and stretching and smoothing themselves out, stockings fell to the floor in little crumpled heaps of purple. An idea began to form in Pip's head . . . Ducking beneath the bats, he picked up a stocking.

'Flora, how good are you at tying knots?' He pulled on the stocking, testing its strength.

Flora was yawning. 'Wilmus taught me, at the feast. I can do the Strangling Snake, the Weaving Worm and – what was the other one? I know – the Un-untieable.'

'Good.' Scooping up a pile of fallen stockings, Pip dumped them on her lap. 'We're going to make a stocking ladder.'

Flora blinked at him and gave another yawn. 'A what?'

'We'll hang it out of the window and climb down it.' Pip's fingers were already busy. 'We'll find Gorbo and then . . . then we'll think of what to do next.'

As the first of the bats separated itself from the washing line and swooped silently away through the window, the children got knotting.

Flora started well but her eyelids were drooping; her fingers fumbled, her knots got muddled, her stockings came apart.

185

She rubbed her eyes. 'I'm so sleepy. Can't I lie down, just for a little while?'

Pip shook his head. 'We have to hurry. We have to find Gorbo before it's too dark.'

'I can't . . .' Flora's head was lolling, her eyes half-closed. Scattering stockings, she keeled over, her head pillowed on her hands. 'Sorry,' she mumbled from behind the fall of her hair. 'So, so sleepy . . .'

'Flora, wake up!' Pip shook her by the shoulders. '*Flora!*' What was wrong with her? He stared down at her. There were gingerbread crumbs around her mouth.

The gingerbread! There was something in the gingerbread!

Pip's eyes flew to the puppy in his cage. 'Tiger! Hey, Tiger!' But he too was fast asleep, nose on paws.

Pip felt suddenly very much alone. The bats had left for the night, streaming through the gap under the thatch, silent as smoke on leathery wings. Only Gubbins remained, watching him through one green slitted eye. How long would it be before Flora woke up? All he could do was keep knotting stockings and hope that he would be able to rouse her when he'd finished the ladder.

186

Stocking after stocking . . . Pip found himself yawning; his eyelids began to close. He sat up with a jolt. *Stupid, you tasted the gingerbread too! You shouldn't have eaten any—!*

He hadn't swallowed more than a mouthful, but he could feel its soporific power beginning to work on him, too strong to resist. He had used up almost all the stockings anyway. He bundled them under the end of the mattress, out of sight, and lay down next to Flora.

'Not for long,' he told himself. 'Just for a little while . . .'

CHAPTER 24½

S ometime later, the door creaked open and Widow Meldrum came in. Holding up her candle, she looked down at the figures on the bed, listening to the sound of their breathing.

'Two little orphans. One small dog,' she counted. Her shadow, in the flickering light, stood straight and tall. She had lost her stoop, as her voice had lost its aged quaver. Her eyes gleamed like amethysts. 'Sweet dreams, sleep tight,' she murmured. 'Don't let the nightmares bite. There'll be time for that later.'

CHAPTER 25

Pip dreamt: he was back in the circus ring, swinging from a trapeze made of purple stockings. Far below stood his father, red-faced and roaring. 'Jump, you stupid little worm!' If he fell, he knew what his father would do to him. Better to stay up there swinging back and forth, back and forth. But the knots weren't strong enough; the stockings were beginning to stretch and fray . . . Pip fell out of one dream and into another, waking in his bed at Sunny Bay with sunlight flooding through the window and the promise of breakfast . . .

When he woke for real the Sunny Bay dream feeling

clung on, warm and comfortable, until he remembered where he was. After the golden sunshine in his dream, the darkness was chilling. Turning his head, he could make out the pale puddle of Flora's hair. Tiger, full of gingerbread crumbs, was snoring in his cage.

Downstairs, a door slammed.

'What happened to you?' Widow Meldrum's voice was mocking. 'You look half-drowned.'

'I don't like trolls, Muzzer. Not nice to poor Golithos. I only asked if she had seen any nice juicy children. She pushed me in the river. Suppose she has already gobbled them?'

'She hasn't,' said Widow Meldrum. 'They're safe upstairs – and they've eaten enough of my gingerbread to keep them asleep till noon.'

Golithos. Foul of breath and fierce of fang. Pip was wide awake now. He wriggled off the mattress and crept to the door, easing it open, willing it not to creak. Dropping down on his stomach, he squirmed to the top of the stairs from where he could see part of the kitchen below. Big boots on the end of a pair of long legs and a head like a moss-grown boulder. Pip recognized the back of that head. He had seen it before, wearing a chauffeur's cap.

Dropping into a chair several sizes too small for him, the giant noticed Baldry seated on the other side of the table, spooning up soup.

'What's that, Muzzer?'

'That, my son, is His Majesty King Kul's very own Idiot.'

'Fool, not Idiot,' objected Baldry. 'Actually, I prefer *Jester* as a job description.'

'Why's it got bells on?' Golithos stared at him. 'What's it doing here?'

'I have been wondering that myself,' said Widow Meldrum, 'What *are* you doing here, Master Jester, apart from drinking my soup and getting in the way? Don't bother telling me that you're helping those children and their Snerg out of the kindness of your heart, because I shall not believe you. Your heart is no kinder than mine.'

'We both know,' said Baldry, 'that the King does not allow strangers in his lands – and the capture of a Snerg is worth seventeen pieces of silver.'

'So haul him off to Banrive and collect your prize,' said

Widow Meldrum. 'Why bring him here?'

'He resisted capture; it was three against one.' Baldry flapped his hands, shooing a cat who had jumped on to his lap. 'I am not a man of violence, so I resolved to use cunning instead. *Get them to the witch*, I thought. *She'll help you.* I don't mind sharing the reward. Twelve pieces of silver for me — he's my Snerg, after all — and five for you. The thing is . . . I would rather not show my face in Banrive just now. I am a wanted man, charged with offences of a . . . dairy-related nature. There was an incident involving butter. And some steps. And some royal behinds. I found it amusing. The King didn't.'

'You have come to the wrong person,' said Widow Meldrum, setting a bowl of soup down in front of her son. 'I am no more welcome in Banrive than you are.'

'The King need not know that you're a witch,' argued Baldry. He eyed her up and down. 'It's a pity that you look quite so . . .'

'Hideous?' Widow Meldrum laughed. 'A loathsome old hag with more warts than poor Mr B.' The toad swivelled its gold-flecked eyes at this, puffing its throat and letting out a lugubrious burp. 'No speaking!' snapped the widow, giving its cage a push to set it swinging. 'You shouldn't judge the fruit by its peel, Master Fool. A beautiful heart may beat beneath an ugly skin . . . and the other way around.'

Picking up a bone-handled mirror from the dresser, she began to pick the warts, one by one, from her chin. She tossed them to the cats who pounced, batting at them with black paws. Finally, she peeled off her pimpled hook of a nose.

'Chicken skin,' explained Widow Meldrum, wiping the grease from her own perfectly straight nose. As she pushed back the hood of her gown her long dark hair fell loose, touched here and there with silver. 'No need to stare, Mr Baldry. My disguise may not be pretty but it's good for business. People are easily fooled – and they'll pay double the price for curses bought from a witch who's properly wizened and warty.' Sitting down, she kicked off the rat slippers and stretched out her legs in their violet stockings. 'Like you, I have good reason not to show my real face. Have a little more of my elderberry cordial, Mr Baldry. Do you know why the King has such a fear of magic?'

Baldry sipped at the glass she handed him. 'I've heard the stories. Mad gabblings about a witch turning his first queen into a frog on their wedding day. Only an idiot would believe . . .' He tailed off, his mouth hanging open as he stared at Widow Meldrum. She was smiling the sort of smile that goes with pleasant memories. 'It's true? It was *you*?'

'She made a very pretty little frog,' said Widow Meldrum, 'with her skinny legs and bulging eyes. Off she hopped into the pond, where I'm sure she was delightfully happy catching flies and laying blobs of frogspawn.'

Baldry took a long gulp of elderberry cordial. 'But . . . *why*?'

Widow Meldrum shrugged. 'Why not? The King could have married me instead. I had a fancy to be queen. I would have ruled Banrive for him – he would have had nothing to do but sit and comb his beard all day. But he wanted little Frog-Face. Such a royal tantrum when he realized what had happened. They'd have flung me in a dungeon but I slipped through their fingers like swamp mist and escaped up into the hills, where I met a rock troll. He let me share his cave – until he stayed out too late one morning. Poor Meldrum. The sun's rays caught him and turned him to stone.'

'Bad luck for the poor fellow,' said Baldry, finishing his cordial and reaching for the bottle.

'Luck had very little to do with it,' said the widow. 'Solid granite between his ears and a face like a fossilized potato. You might as well hold a conversation with a tombstone. I could not put up with that for ever. I coaxed him out one night to help me count the stars.' She laughed. 'He couldn't get past three, poor blockhead, but I kept him there until the sun came up. He didn't stand a chance. What are *you* gawping at?'

The giant was staring at her, a spoonful of soup halfway to his mouth. 'Muzzer killed Farzer?'

She patted him on the shoulder. 'Don't look at me like that. I took care of you, didn't I? I raised my little Golithos into a fine ogre. When you were grown, I sent you down from the hills to make a nuisance of yourself and give all the Kelp children nightmares.'

'Nice children. Juicy.' Golithos had a shred of boiled leaf hanging from his top lip. He sighed, remembering happier times. 'But then the other wickedy witch stopped me. Terrible pains in my biters – such stabbings and throbbings and tweakings in my crunchers and munchers if I so much as dribble over a morsel of meat. Turnips,' said Golithos, almost tearfully, 'are not the same.'

'Speaking of children,' remarked Baldry thoughtfully. 'Those two upstairs . . . if we fattened them up and padded them out a bit, they could pass as Snergs. The King won't know the difference – he has more beard than sense. That would be a reward of three times seventeen pieces of silver, which is . . . quite a lot.'

'I fear that we won't be seeing your Snerg again.' Widow Meldrum filled up his glass. 'He too has eaten my gingerbread. You need your wits about you in the Distressful Swamp. Fall asleep there, alone in the dark, and you are very unlikely to see the morning. Your bones will have been picked clean long before sunrise.'

Baldry frowned. 'I thought you sent him out to fetch you your weeds?'

Laughing, Widow Meldrum picked up her umbrella. 'Don't you understand, Master Fool, that I am no more to be trusted than you are? I have plenty of mandrake root in my store cupboard; I don't need any more. Nor do I need a

Snerg bobbing about and getting in the way. The children are another matter. I'm not handing the girl over to you, or to King Kul. She is part of my plan.'

'What plan?' Baldry was curious.

'A little matter of revenge.' Widow Meldrum sat idly twirling her umbrella. Her eyes rested on her gingerbread house and all the little screaming marzipan faces. 'All those years up in the hills, with the trolls and the goblins, I was waiting. When enough time had passed for the world to have forgotten me, I came back down and set up my little business here. But I have a promise still to keep . . .' Sparks shot from the spike of her umbrella; flames flickered, lilac and magenta, around the gingerbread walls. Several of the little marzipan figures melted into sticky puddles. 'I never get tired of doing that,' said the widow dreamily.

Baldry's eyes were suddenly sly. 'What if King Kul found out that the poor old woman living on the edge of the swamp is the same witch who be-frogged his bride? Suppose someone were to tell him? What's it worth, to keep my mouth shut?' Sneering, he drained his glass. 'Poor old Mother Meldrum – not such a wise woman after all, are you? You've told me rather too much!'

'I have, haven't I?' she agreed. 'What a pity. I've so enjoyed our little chat.'

'What . . . ?' Baldry was trying to stand up but his face was suddenly clammy with sweat. He swayed on his feet before collapsing back down.

'Only a fool drinks three glasses of a witch's cordial,' said Widow Meldrum.

As the umbrella snapped open, Pip's view was blocked by a circle of purple roses. A *pop*, a wisp of mauve smoke . . . and a croak. The widow folded the umbrella up again. Baldry's brightly coloured hose and jerkin lay on the floor in a crumpled heap. Something moved. A cat patted at it. A tiny red and yellow frog hopped under the table. With every hop came a faint jingle.

Widow Meldrum shooed the cat away. 'Don't touch it, Sister Gutspill; it is very likely poisonous. A very unpleasant young man. And undoubtedly a fool – he seems to have swallowed one of his own bells.'

CHAPTER 26

'Flora, come on, wake up – you've *got* to! We have to rescue Gorbo before he has his bones picked by goblins, or his brains sucked by snotril worms, or gets squeazelled by mud-whatsits. *Flora!*'

Pip had already tied one end of the stocking ladder to the bats' beam, letting the other end dangle out of the window. Leaning out as far as he dared, he could see the bottom: it was near enough to the ground. It took a lot of shaking to get Flora to open her eyes and pay attention, but Pip managed to heave her on to her feet at last. Outside, the darkness of night was beginning to separate into shadows.

The children caught their breath as one of the shadows swooped under the thatch, skimming the top of their heads. The bats were coming home to roost.

Pulling himself up, Pip swung one leg over the sill. It was an easy matter for a wiry circus child to swarm down a swinging ladder, even with a snoring puppy tucked inside his shirt. Flora was less willing – she was still bleary with sleep and had not grown up accustomed to dangling in thin air – but the idea of being left behind frightened her more than the risk of falling. For a nasty moment it seemed as if she might stick, wedged tight in the window. Some urgent wriggling and the thought of Gorbo, alone and in danger, pushed her through. Moments later, she thudded down beside Pip.

'*Downhill until your feet get wet*,' said Pip, remembering the directions Widow Meldrum had given Gorbo. 'Come on.'

'My feet are squelching,' complained Flora a little while later. The effects of the gingerbread had left her feeling queasy and with a headache.

'Squelching is good,' Pip encouraged her. 'It means we're in the right place.' Glancing over his shoulder, he decided not to tell Flora that they were being followed, tracked by a long-legged shadow with a crooked tail.

The mushy ground made small popping, sucking sounds beneath them. It was hard to see very far through the wreathing mist. Pip was trying not to think about snotril worms crawling across his skin, looking for a way to wriggle inside him. More than once he thought he heard muffled giggles coming from the reeds, and glimpsed the gleam of watching eyes . . .

They called for Gorbo as loudly as they dared, in hissing whispers. No answer came.

'The bog-goblins have taken him.' Flora wasn't in the mood to be cheerful. She hugged the sleeping Tiger, to make herself feel better. 'Or the mud-squeazels have dragged him down. Or—'

'No, they haven't.' Pip wouldn't let it be true. 'Look, there's a butterfly . . . two, three . . . lots of them.'

Wings fluttered around them, patterned black and green.

'*Ow!*' One of them had landed on Flora's neck. She tried

to brush it away, but it had fastened itself to her throat. 'They're *vampire* butterflies! Get it *off* me!'

Pip plucked the creature off, not liking the feel of its hairy little body between his fingers. There were more of them now, swarming in a cloud around Flora, drawn by the bead of blood glistening on her skin. Pip shrugged off his Snerg waistcoat and flapped it at them. Ducking their heads, swatting at their necks, the children ran – as well as they could on such swampy ground. Every now and then, one of them would put a foot wrong, sinking up to their knees; while the other had to stop and pull them out.

At last they left the vampire butterflies behind. The mist had thinned, and the ground felt firmer. They had slowed down to catch their breath when the early-morning silence was suddenly, shockingly, split by a shrill wail.

Pip winced. 'What's *that?*'

'I think,' panted Flora, 'I *think* you've just trodden on a howling slug.'

The noise went on and on, filling their ears and chilling their blood, like the cry of a wolf baying at the moon. Tiger woke, whimpering, from his enchanted sleep. Another slug answered, then another, the sound swelling until it became unbearable. Desperate to escape, the children took to their heels again. They kept running until they broke out of the swamp, on to hard ground. With sorrowful slug song still ringing in their ears, they did not hear the hoof beats until it was too late.

'Snerg!' bawled a voice.

'Two of the little scoundrels! Quick – don't let them get away!' shouted another.

The children veered back towards the swamp, but hooves were already thundering down on them. Strong arms caught hold of them, hoisting them up into the air. Before they knew it, they were both in the saddle, breathless and gasping, each with a mail-clad arm clamped like a vice across their chest. As the horses wheeled around, the armoured figure at their head raised his sword, whirling it above his head.

'A calamity upon the heads of all Snergs!' he cried. 'Onwards, brave Kelps! To Banrive!'

CHAPTER 27

High in a tall tree on the other side of the river, a small person folded up a brass telescope and began to climb down through the branches. On the ground, a group of elderly men in large boots sat on a fallen tree trunk, resting their sore feet and aching knees while they chewed on Miss Scadging's cucumber sandwiches.

Pompo dropped out of the tree and handed the telescope back to Captain Vanderdecken.

'Did you see anything?' asked Queen Mercy, removing an inquisitive ostrich beak from her own sandwich.

'Noodles, your Majesty,' announced Pompo, straightening

his feathered cap. 'Dressed in iron, waving spears and riding spotted gallopers with flowing manes and tails. I rigorously regret to report, O Quaquaversal Queen, that I saw them snatch up the half-Noodles and thunder away with them in a most ferocious and fulminatory manner.'

'Kelp soldiers,' said the Queen grimly. 'Was Gorbo with them?'

Pompo shook his head. 'There was a woman. Long and straight, even for a Noodle, wrapped in a shawl of porphyric purple. She came out of the swamp just as they rode off.'

'She who wears purple . . .' murmured the Queen. 'So it's true: she has come back. There's no time to lose – we must cross this river. It's a lucky thing we brought the Chief Inventor with us. Is the Snerg-Launching Contraption ready?'

The Queen's Chief Inventor was an elderly Snerg with an extra-large head, to fit in a lifetime of clever ideas, and a brow furrowed by thinking-wrinkles. Peering at some diagrams she had scratched in the earth, she was doing some last minute calculations on her fingers. Above her towered her latest invention – a triangle of wooden planks supporting a long beam, from one end of which hung something like a large string bag.

'Will it work?' enquired the Queen.

'It can't not work,' said the Chief Inventor. 'It's Physics. Physics always works – it's people who don't. The Designated Weights will climb the tree.' She pointed at two cheerful and especially roly-poly Snergs. 'They will take up their position on that branch *there*. At my signal they will fall off the branch, landing on that platform *there*. The beam will then tip, the launching cradle will be released and the Projectile will fly across the river. Probably.'

'Where is the Projectile?' asked the Queen.

The Projectile turned out to be Wilmus, the shy young Snerg who had sat next to Flora at the feast. He was wearing a string harness, with a long coil of rope wrapped around his stomach, and was looking a little anxious.

'The end of that rope is tied around the tree,' explained the Chief Inventor, 'so that even if my calculations are not quite correct and he were to land in the river, we could reel him back in.'

'Before the crocopotami get to him, or after?' wondered Pompo.

'I'd rather it was before,' offered Wilmus. 'If nobody minds.'

'It might be a good idea to stick a saucepan on his head,' advised Captain Vanderdecken, who had experience with dangerous situations. 'In case of unexpected bumpings.'

So a saucepan was found and jammed on to Wilmus's head. It was rather too large and came down over his eyes.

'All the better,' the Queen encouraged him. 'What you can't see you don't know about, and what you don't know about can't worry you.'

All that could be seen of Wilmus – which wasn't very much – did not look totally sure about this but he let himself be bundled into the string launching cradle, where – on the Chief Inventor's instructions – he curled himself into a tight ball. Giggling, the Designated Weights climbed their tree. The Chief Inventor cleared her throat and began the countdown.

'5 . . . 4 . . . 3 . . . 2 . . . 1 . . . *now!*'

The Weights fell obediently off their branch. The beam

tipped. The launching cradle whirled up. A small, round shape whizzed through the air, like one of the *Flying Dutchman*'s cannon balls. Everybody held their breath . . .

'He's made it!' The Captain had his telescope to his eye.

A cheer went up. On the other side of the river, a shape could be seen dangling from a pine tree, where Wilmus's rope had caught. Being a Snerg, he was quite at home in the branches, even with a saucepan jammed over his eyes, and had soon righted himself. Feeling his way, he looped his end of the rope around the pine trunk and pulled it tight so that it stretched, like a giant's washing line, across the river. Hand over hand, Wilmus began to make his way back. The watchers on the bank gasped and murmured as the water below him began to boil and bubble. With much thrashing and splashing and flashing of scales, a crocopotamus reared up – green, gargantuan and ghastly. Any Snerg falling into its cavernous jaws would have dropped straight down into its stomach without even touching the sides. Happily for Wilmus, his toes stayed out of reach.

'Well done, Wilmus,' approved the Queen, when he was safely on solid ground again. 'I award you the Brazen

Nutmeg for Bravery and appoint you my Royal Knotsman. Somebody find some butter,' she ordered, as Wilmus blushed pink under his saucepan. 'Get that thing off his head.'

'I hope that rope is strong enough to hold us all,' said Captain Vanderdecken. 'Your Snergs are great of heart and capacious of stomach, ma'am, but my men are rather heavier.'

'Snergs know their string, sir,' the Queen reassured him. 'That rope is wound with pixie thread and spider silk. It would hold a herd of huffalumps without fraying.'

Pompo was trying to persuade the Queen's ostrich into one of the special flying harnesses designed by the Chief Inventor for the purpose of getting large flightless birds across rivers. 'I can't help wondering about Gorbo,' he remarked, dodging a snapping beak. 'He may be inexorably and ineradicably intellectually impeded – that is to say, he's a bit of a nitwit – but I've known him since we were Snerglets. I wouldn't wish the poor pudding-head in impassable peril.'

The Queen sighed. 'I fear the worst,' she admitted, 'but who knows? Gorbo may yet surprise us all.'

In which Gorbo
tries, and fails,
to be heroic and the
Expeditionary Force
arrives at the Court of the
Kelps. Much is explained,
including the true identity
of Widow Meldrum's toad
and which witch is which.

CHAPTER 28

Somewhere in the swamp, Gorbo woke from a deep sleep. He had spent an uncomfortable evening wandering about, pulling up plants at random in the hope that they might be mandrakes. A mud-squeazel had done its best, wrapping itself around his ankle and trying to drag him down. When Gorbo pointed an arrow at it, it sank, bubbling, back into the mud. The bog-goblins had picked up his scent and came slipping through the reeds, licking their lips and gibbering to each other. But Gorbo – to keep out the cold and the loneliness – had kept himself company by humming a little hum. Every now and then, the hum had grown words.

With a bing and a bong, I shall sing you my song,
Though the tune isn't right and the words are all wrong . . .

Not much of a song, but it was enough. Goblins cannot stand the sound of cheerfulness. Sulking, they kept their distance.

With enough oddly shaped roots to fill the bottom of his sack, Gorbo began to feel peckish. Remembering the gingerbread in his pocket, he looked about him for a dry tussock to sit on while he ate it. It was not long before he was curled in a ball, fast asleep. The goblins came creeping back, but their rubbery little nostrils sniffed out the smell of the gingerbread crumbs. Pausing only to steal the arrows from his quiver, they scuttled back to their damp holes. They knew the smell of magic when they met it.

It was a lucky thing for Gorbo, when Pip trod on the howling slug. The noise broke into his dreams and roused him just in time. The ground had been oozing and glooping around him as he slept, drawing him further and further down. Soon it would have swallowed him up completely and that would have been that. Snorting bog mud out of his nose, Gorbo rolled out of his deadly bed.

'A fine place to fall asleep, you goof,' he rebuked himself. 'And a fine moment too, just when you had an important job to do.' He sighed. 'Aunt Flumper's right about you: Gorbo the Gump, irredeemably irresponsible and a sad disgrace to the race of Snergs.'

Peering inside his sack, he inspected the little heap of roots he had collected. He poked one; it gave a bad-tempered squeak.

'Must be mandrake,' decided Gorbo. 'Come on then, let's get you back to old Widow Meldrum. With a little bit of luck, she'll be cooking up some breakfast by now.'

'Kidnapped?' Gorbo stared at Widow Meldrum, his eyes full of horror. 'What do you mean?'

'Stolen by Kelp soldiers.' Widow Meldrum was back in her peasant's cloak and rat slippers, stooped and quavering. 'Bad things happen to naughty, ungrateful children who run away from their friends. I fear for their safety once King Kul has them in his clutches.'

'I should never have left them!' cried Gorbo. 'You said

you'd look after them.'

'And *you* said that you would bring me mandrakes,' snapped Widow Meldrum, tipping the contents of the sack on to the kitchen table. 'I can't put a troll to sleep with common swamp parsnips.'

'Never mind trolls!' exclaimed Gorbo. 'That doesn't matter now – I can't go home without those children! What sort of a friend would do that? Whatever would Miss Watkyns say?'

'Oh, Miss Watkyns . . .' Widow Meldrum spat on the dying embers in the fireplace. Bright fuchsia sparks shot across the kitchen, very much upsetting the cat snoozing in front of the grate. 'We mustn't forget about *her.*'

'I must go after them,' declared Gorbo. 'At once!'

'They'll be halfway to Banrive by now,' Widow Meldrum told him. 'It's no use you hurtling out of here like a bee-stung bullock. You wouldn't even get through the gates before somebody seized you and claimed their seventeen pieces of silver. There's no need to look as if the sky is falling,' She patted his shoulder. 'All is not lost. I can help you. Wait there.'

She was gone some minutes, leaving Gorbo to pace the kitchen floor tearing at his hair and tripping over cats. When she returned, she brought with her three packages wrapped in tattered cloth.

'I have never shown these to a living soul,' announced Widow Meldrum. 'They are very ancient and possessed of powerful magic – too powerful for most people. But I can see that you are a Snerg of great character and courage, born to do heroic deeds.'

'Ummm,' said the hero, a bit uncertainly.

'This,' said the witch, unwrapping the first parcel, 'is the Cloak of Invisibility. Put it on, and you will disappear.'

'Some of it's already disappeared,' remarked Gorbo. 'It's got a lot of holes in it.'

'I said it was old,' snapped Widow Meldrum. 'No, you can't try it on now.' She whisked it out of Gorbo's reach. 'The magic only works once, for any one person. If you waste your turn, you won't get another – and you will need it if you want to get into King Kul's Palace. Secondly . . .' She unfolded the second package. '. . . the Switch of Doom.'

'It's a twig,' said Gorbo.

'It *looks* like a twig,' Widow Meldrum corrected him. 'But when you smite with it, it will become a blade of the brightest, sharpest metal. A blade that cannot miss its target.'

'What is its target?' Gorbo was looking uneasy.

'King Kul, of course!'

Gorbo took a step backwards. 'I'm not really the smiting sort . . .'

'I thought you had a noble heart,' Widow Meldrum reproached him. 'I thought you wanted to rescue those children.'

'More than anything,' Gorbo assured her. 'But . . . I hoped I could settle it with King Kul in a "hello, pleased to meet you, been a bit of a misunderstanding, no hard feelings" sort of a way.'

'Not possible,' said the widow. 'The King is a brute. If you don't smite him first, he'll have your head rolling about the floor in the wink of an eye. It is your only chance to save those children.'

Gorbo swallowed. 'Supposing I do smite him? Then what?'

'Then,' said Widow Meldrum, unrolling the third

package, 'you slip on the Sandals of Swiftness – and you run. Not too fast, not too far – with these on your feet, you will find yourself in deepest Africa or at the North Pole before you know it. Their magic is very strong but – like the cloak and dagger – you may use them only once. Do not be tempted to try them before you need them, or the power is lost to you.'

'But,' said Gorbo, 'if I run away, what will happen to the children?'

'Leave that to me,' said Widow Meldrum. 'I will take care of them. Come, there is no time to lose. You must harness Mr Horniman to the cart – he will get us there as quickly as he can.'

'Oh,' said Gorbo, feeling a little braver. 'You're coming with me?'

'Of course I am.' Widow Meldrum smiled. 'Do you think I'd miss this? Not for all the gold in Banrive!'

CHAPTER 29

It was market day in Banrive. As the soldiers clattered in through the city gates, the sight of their prisoners caused a stir.

'Snergs! Sir Percival's netted a brace of Snergs!'

'Filthy dumplings!'

Somebody hurled a tomato; it caught Flora on the shoulder. Pip caught a flying onion and threw it back.

'Vicious!' muttered the crowd. 'Savage little beasts!'

The children were bruised and aching from being jolted in the saddle. Now rough hands lifted them down and they were tossed over armoured shoulders, to the sound of jeers and whistles and cries of 'Off with their heads! Throw them to the centipedes!'

'Quick march!' barked a voice. 'To the King!'

King Kul was in his banqueting hall. Even at breakfast he was a regal figure, long of beard and generous of stomach. His crown flashed with jewels, his sky-blue velvet cloak was stitched with gold and his knickerbockers were a dashing shrimp-pink. Around him sat his royal children. After his first bride hopped into the palace lily pond, he had spent many years as a lonesome bachelor. Just as frogs must have tadpoles, however, kings must have princelings and princesses. Time passed and the King had married a new queen. Unfortunately, she had taken a serious tumble down Baldry's buttered steps, all the way to the bottom. The royal doctors had wrapped her in bandages and told her to stay in bed. Without their mother there to keep an eye on them, the royal children were sadly out of hand and spreading far too much jam on their muffins.

Crown, thrones, goblets, porridge bowls – everything at the High Table gleamed gold. The King's courtiers sat on long benches to either side, while servants bustled in between, balancing platters and pitchers. Tall Kelp hounds with waving tails nosed for scraps. The King had a pageboy beside him, waiting with a golden comb, ready to brush the muffin crumbs from his long silver beard. On his other side, a minstrel strummed a lute. King Kul liked to begin every day with the Kelp national anthem.

To be a Kelp is much the best,
For Kelps are better than the rest.
Banrive glitters, bright with gold,
Damsels fair and knights so bold.
Side by side, we'll fight off dangers,
Scurril Snergs and other strangers . . .

The guards in the doorway uncrossed their lances to let Sir Percival and his prisoners through.

'Snergs, Your Majesty.' The knight bowed. 'We came upon them skulking on the edge of the Distressful Swamp.'

At his signal, Flora and Pip were dropped on the hard stone floor.

There were whispers, and a rustling of velvet and silks, from the courtiers' benches.

'Snergs!'

'Real live ones! And a Snerg-hound!'

'Do they bite?'

'I heard they were poisonous . . .'

'Tie them up!'

'Throw them in the dungeons!'

'Off with their heads!'

'We're not Snergs,' said Pip.

'They can talk!' exclaimed a lady in a complicated head-dress. 'I thought that Snergs could only speak in grunts.'

'I heard that they live in trees,' said another. 'Like animals.'

'And look at the clothes they wear!' said a third, smoothing her own satin skirts and shuddering at Flora's breeches.

'They don't look much like the statue,' remarked the youngest princess, who was trying to stuff a raisin up the smallest prince's nose.

Everybody's eyes swivelled towards the corner of the hall, where a bronze Kelp sat astride his bronze horse, about to thrust a spear into his enemy. The enemy was short and stout, showing long fangs in an evil leer as he tried to chew the horse's leg off.

'If that's meant to be a Snerg,' said Flora critically, 'it doesn't look anything like one.'

Sir Percival cleared his throat. 'If the statue looks nothing like a Snerg, and the prisoners look not much like the statue – does that not indeed prove their veritable Snerg-ness?'

There was a murmur of agreement. King Kul peered down at Pip and Flora.

'Speak, dumplings! What are you doing in my lands? Were you sent as spies, or are you thieves, planning to steal our royal treasure?'

'Neither,' said Pip. 'We got here by mistake. We don't want to be here. We want to get back to Sunny Bay.'

'Home,' echoed Flora. 'We want to go home.'

'Lies, Your Majesty,' said Sir Percival. 'I suggest that we try suspending them over a pit of sabre-toothed centipedes. We will lower them in slowly. By the time they are in up to their ankles, they will have confessed their wicked plots.'

Everybody seemed to think that this was a sensible idea. Sir Percival barked an order. Heavy hands grasped the children's collars.

'No! Let me *go*!' Flora squirmed and kicked, with Tiger growling in her arms.

'Wait . . .' Half-dangling from a mailed fist, Pip looked straight at King Kul. 'He said you'd be fooled.'

The king's silver brows snapped together in a frown. 'Fooled? Me? Who dared say so?'

'Your jester, Baldry,' said Pip. 'He wanted to claim the reward for capturing us. He said that you had more beard than sense and that it would be easy to trick you into believing we were Snergs.'

The silence stretched out. The courtiers held their breath. So did Pip and Flora.

'Nobody,' said the King at last, '*nobody* plays tricks on King Kul of Banrive. I am not so easily bamboozled, whatever that jackanapes of a jester may think! Not for a single *moment* did I really suppose that you were Snergs. Sir Percival was fooled of course, poor fellow, but not I. Snergs, indeed! Ha ha! What an idea! Anyone with any sense at all can see that you are far too *narrow.*'

'Ha ha! Snergs! A ridiculous idea!' sniggered the courtiers, all in a great hurry to show that they had more sense than Sir Percival.

'But,' said Sir Percival, 'they wear Snerg clothes. And if not Snergs . . . what *are* they?'

'Strangers!' The courtiers stopped sniggering. 'Not Kelps.' 'Not one of us!' 'Different!' 'What are they?'

'Orphans,' said Flora, heaving a long and tragic sigh. 'Superfluous and Accidentally Parentless Children. Lost and lonely. And terribly, terribly hungry . . .' she added, eyeing the royal breakfast.

'Children!' 'They're only children!' The mutter rippled through the courtiers. 'Poor little lost things . . .'

There was another long pause while everyone looked at King Kul, thoughtfully twiddling his beard. *Please*, thought Pip. *Please not the centipedes.*

The King clapped his hands together, making everybody jump.

'More chairs!' he commanded. 'We will have no more talk of centipedes. Let these young people be washed and dressed, in something less . . . Snerg-ish, then they will join us at breakfast. Sir Percival, take your men away and find them something better to do than arresting innocent children!'

Pip and Flora were whisked away, scrubbed and brushed and squeezed into clothes borrowed from the Kelp princes and princesses. Pip had a velvet cape over one shoulder and a matching hat with a feather that tickled his ear. Flora kicked at the skirts of her silk dress, embroidered with bees. Her hat was tall and pointed, with a fluttering veil, and kept slipping sideways. Her shoes were too tight and she missed her Snerg breeches.

Pip looked her up and down and grinned. 'You look like a doll. That's a very stupid hat.'

Flora scowled. 'You can't talk,' she retorted. 'You should see yourself – you look absolutely ridiculous!'

Back in the banqueting hall, places had been laid for them at the High Table. So keen was King Kul to prove that he had never believed they were Snergs, he got off his throne to heap their golden plates with his own royal hand. Picking out a particularly plump muffin for Flora, he was bending over to butter it for her when something unexpected happened . . .

CHAPTER 30

A small, round figure in a moth-eaten cloak dived beneath the guards' crossed lances and hurtled towards the High Table. Taking the steps two at a time, it raised a long, whippy twig – and brought it down hard on King Kul's backside.

Jaws dropped. Dogs barked. Chairs scraped. Golden cutlery clattered. The King let out a bellow.

'Gorbo!' cried the children.

'Don't just stand there!' the King howled at the guards. 'Do something! I'm being assassinated!'

The assassin was behaving strangely: he seemed to be changing his shoes.

'Gorbo, run!' Pip begged him. 'Get away!'

'No need to worry about me,' said Gorbo, tugging at a sandal. 'As soon as I get these Sandals of Swiftness on, I'll be gone in no time. Although,' he added, looking doubtfully at the Switch of Doom and then at King Kul, who did not seem to be at all dead, 'it is not going quite as she said it would. I'm not at all sure this Cloak of Invisibility is working and – oh dear,' said Gorbo sadly, as the guards seized him by the arms.

'Lock him up!' exploded the King, clutching his injured behind. 'Feed him to the centipedes! Summon the Grand High Executioner!'

'The Executioner!' 'The Executioner!' The courtiers were in an uproar. 'Chop off its head!'

'There is no Executioner, Your Majesty,' admitted one of the guards. 'There hasn't been a head chopped off for so long, he retired. He hung up his axe and grows roses now, in a little cottage down by the river.'

'In that case I hope the centipedes are hungry,' said the King peevishly. 'Wrap the rogue in chains – and mind he doesn't bite your fingers off. You can see he's vicious.'

'Please don't hurt him!' begged Pip. 'He's not vicious – he's Gorbo.'

'It was the witch,' added Flora. 'She told him to do it.'

'Nonsense!' King Kul's silver eyebrows bristled. 'There are no witches in Banrive! *Now* what's the matter? Can a king not eat his breakfast in peace?'

An armoured soldier had clanked to a halt in the doorway, rather out of breath. 'A message for His Majesty. Urgent. Strangers at the gates. Small people riding monstrous birds.'

'Snergs . . .' The whisper rustled around the room again.

'They have others with them,' said the soldier. 'Venerable grandfathers in big boots. Sir Percival has challenged them, but they refuse to fight. They wish to speak with Your Majesty.'

'Well, I don't wish to speak with *them*,' said the King, crossly. 'Don't let them in.'

'No, Your Majesty,' agreed the soldier. 'Except – I'm afraid that they let themselves in. The birds,' he added, 'are *very* large. One of them trod on Sir Percival's foot.'

'Then let them come and explain this, if they can.' The

King waved an irritable hand at Gorbo. 'If they can't . . .
we'll lock the whole lot of them in the dungeons and roast
their birds for our dinner.'

Pompo came first, blasting a fanfare on his horn.

'Whatever did they want to bring *him* for?' grumbled
Gorbo, so cocooned in chains that only his head and feet
could be seen sticking out at either end.

'Her Marvellous Majesty Queen Mercy – Most Porten-
tous, Proscipient and Pearlescent of Potentates, Sapient,
Scintillating and Superlative Sovereign of the Snergs and all
their Surroundings,' announced Pompo. 'Also, Captain
Vanderdecken and the Most Cantankerously Confusticated
and Carpophagous Crew of the *Flying Dutchman.*'

A ripple ran through the Kelps as the Queen's ostrich
stepped in among them. Queen Mercy sat very straight on
his back in her tall bird headdress, flanked by her riders.
Beside her, Captain Vanderdecken led his crew forward with
bristling whiskers and the heavy tramp of boots.

The King of the Kelps and the Queen of the Snergs
bowed stiffly to each other. The Captain and his men raised

their hats and clicked their heels.

'Hail,' said the King, very formally.

'We come in peace.' Queen Mercy's bright glance swept the hall and found Pip and Flora. 'We seek these children, so we may return them to where they belong. And one other – one of my own, temporarily mislaid.'

'I suppose you mean *him*?' said King Kul bitterly, pointing at Gorbo.

'You seem to have got tangled up with some chains, Gorbo,' remarked Queen Mercy, with a sigh. 'What trouble are you in now?'

'Wilful Damage to the Royal Person,' complained the King. 'I was regaling these children with kindness and muffins when I suffered an unprovoked assault upon my sit-upon. There will be bruising, and extra cushions required on the throne.'

'Gorbo was trying to rescue us.' Flora rushed to his defence. 'There was a bit of a muddle . . . but he was very brave.'

'*If* your idea of bravery is attacking a fellow from behind when he's buttering a muffin,' sniffed King Kul.

'It was all the witch's fault,' said Pip. 'Widow Meldrum.'

'I told you – there are no witches here,' snapped the King. 'Any kind of magic is forbidden. Meldrum? Never heard of her. Don't know the woman.'

'Yes, you do,' asserted Pip. 'She was the one who . . .' He stopped; something told him King Kul might be sensitive about what had happened to his bride.

'What?' demanded the King. 'She was the one who what?'

Pip took a deep breath. 'She was the one who turned your wife into . . . into a . . . a frog.'

There was a moment of shocked silence. The courtiers coughed and shuffled. All eyes slid towards King Kul. He was frowning so hard his eyebrows nearly climbed down his nose. Puffing out his stomach, he rose up on to his toes and tugged at his beautifully curled beard.

'My first wife did suffer an accident of an amphibious nature,' he conceded sternly. 'But the twisted heart that cursed her – her name was not Meldrum. Her name was Watkyns.'

CHAPTER 31

Many surprising things had happened to Pip and Flora since they left Sunny Bay. Perhaps the most surprising thing of all was the idea of Miss Watkyns turning anybody into a frog.

'No.' Pip shook his head. 'Miss Watkyns doesn't even *believe* in witches. And even supposing she could, she'd never be the turn-you-into-a-frog sort.'

'That,' said Flora, 'would *definitely* be against the rules.'

'Miss Watkyns is a lady of impeccable manners and respectability.' Captain Vanderdecken's beard was jutting at a belligerent angle. 'Any man who speaks of her with disrespect must answer to me and my men!' Glaring at King Kul, he reached for his musket. Faithful to their leader, the crew fumbled for theirs. There was a clash of lances as the guards leapt to attention.

'Wait!' ordered Queen Mercy, reining in her sidling, stamping ostrich. 'Lower your weapons; you are disgruntling my birds. As first course must come before pudding, so explanation should always come before a fight. That is the Snerg way. The explanation in this case is perfectly simple. Gorbo will give it to you.'

'Who? What? Me?' Wrapped in his chains, Gorbo looked alarmed.

'Tell them,' Queen Mercy encouraged him, 'what you found on the beach that day.'

'Oh, *that* . . . that was a long time ago,' said Gorbo. 'Not so long in Snerg years, but I have noticed that Noodle time skips and fidgets along. I had wandered out of the woods – it was one of those follow-your-nose-and-see-where-it-takes-you sort of days. My nose had taken me to the beach at Sunny Bay, to gather shells. I had a pocketful of cowries and was just blowing on rather a fine conch when I noticed a tin box, bobbing about out there on the waves. You should never ignore boxes – they might have biscuits in. This one was making noises, so I waded out to bring it in to shore. Not biscuits. Babies. Two little pink shrimps, wrapped in a tablecloth.'

'Don't believe it,' said King Kul. 'Never heard of such a thing. Who puts babies out to sea in a box?'

'I could tell they were Noodles,' Gorbo went on. 'Funny, spidery little things. One so quiet, looking up at me with such solemn eyes. The other one was squalling, angry as a stormy sea. No names, no anything to call their own except for a little bead necklace each. I wanted to keep them, to take them home to the Snergs, but it was a day's journey through the woods. Little creatures need milk and I had nothing to give them except string and shells. So . . . I put them in a safe place. There was a house in Sunny Bay, behind a high wall: I knew they kept children there, ones that had nowhere else to go. They would be looked after there, I thought, so I carried the box up the cliff and left it at the gates.' Gorbo drooped miserably in his chains. 'Cold-hearted, crinkle-witted villain of a Snerg!' he berated himself. 'I didn't *know* . . .'

'The orphanage at Sunny Bay was a different place in those days.' Queen Mercy took up the tale. 'Dark and miserable – ruled by the worst of Noodles, the sort that enjoys cruelty and pain. His name was Adolphus Bunphatt. Rumours of the unhappiness inside those walls had reached the Land of the Snergs. When Gorbo told me what he had done, I worried for those Noodlings. Snerg hands had lifted them from the water: how could we abandon them? As the years went by, I sent Snergs to do odd jobs at the orphanage so they could bring me news. It was always the same – two girls, alike as two beans on the outside but very different on the inside. One child – Felicia – was calm and good and kept out of trouble. The other – Malicia – broke every rule she could. The more she was punished, the angrier and more troublesome she became.

'One night, fifteen Noodle years after Gorbo first found them, a fire broke out in the orphanage. It was Felicia who raised the alarm and led the children to safety. Afterwards, Malicia was nowhere to be found. She had disappeared – and so had Adolphus Bunphatt. It was presumed that they had met their end in the flames.'

Pip frowned, thinking back to the witch's kitchen: the cats and the gingerbread house and the toad in its cage. He remembered the red and yellow frog hopping under the table, as King Kul's bride had once hopped into the lily pond. How many other people had the witch pointed her purple umbrella at? *And where did she get that toad?*

'I don't think Mr Bunphatt met his end – not exactly.' Pip shivered. 'I think – I'm pretty sure she turned him into a toad.'

Beside him, Flora drew in her breath. 'Mr B . . . !'

'I'm not saying it's right to go around turning people into toads,' granted Queen Mercy, 'but some people do not deserve to be what they are. If you had known Adolphus Bunphatt in his Noodle form, you might feel that he got what he deserved. It was Malicia who set the place ablaze, of course. She wanted her sister to run away with her, but Felicia would not leave the other children to burn in their beds. She remains at the orphanage still. You children know her as Miss Watkyns. As for the *other* Miss Watkyns, news reached us at last that she was very much alive – she had crossed the river and was in Kelp lands.'

'I don't want to talk about that woman.' King Kul was sulky. 'I have spent years trying to forget what she did. How would you like it, on *your* wedding day? Watching your bride hop away on her little webbed feet, splish-sploshing into the pond? And that witch – she just stood there laughing. I should have fed her to the centipedes or locked her in my deepest dungeon and melted down the key. I won't have her back again. I won't!' He thumped the table, setting the gold cups and plates clattering and making all the courtiers jump. 'If what you say is true, then Sir Percival must ride with all speed to arrest her. She will not escape my wrath a second time!'

'She's not alone,' Pip warned him. 'There's Golithos too. *Foul of breath and fierce of fang.* He's her son.'

'Golithos?' King Kul frowned. 'Wasn't that the fellow who made a nuisance of himself some years ago? Things went missing. Cows. Sheep. Children.'

'He troubled the Snergs also,' said Queen Mercy. 'But he was greedy; he went too far – all the way to Sunny Bay. Miss Watkyns caught him peering over the orphanage walls. She could not allow that, so she . . . persuaded him to try a change of diet.'

'But . . .' Pip frowned, trying to remember what he had overheard in Widow Meldrum's kitchen. 'Golithos was moaning about how he had to give up eating children because a wicked witch put a toothache spell on him . . .' He tailed off as the pieces fitted together inside his head. 'There was another witch,' he said slowly, not sure if he believed his own words. 'But she wasn't wicked. She was—

Flora said it for him. 'She was Miss Watkyns!'

Queen Mercy nodded. 'Both girls grew up with special talents. Malicia always enjoyed using hers to make mischief; Felicia locked hers away for moments of desperate need. An infantivorous ogre in an orphanage is one of those moments. She did as she thought best – she didn't know, of course,' added the Queen, 'that this particular ogre was her nephew.'

'She could have turned him into anything she liked, and the best she could think of was a vegetarian?' Flora was disappointed.

'It was after that,' went on the Queen, 'that Miss Watkyns

shut the gate.'

'What gate?' asked Pip.

'You walked through it yourselves, although all you saw was a split yew tree,' the Queen told him. 'How do you think you reached the Land of the Snergs? The gate stays locked, on Miss Watkyns's orders, to keep two worlds apart. We Snergs hold the key.'

'How do you lock a gate you can't see?' wondered Flora.

'With words,' said the Queen. 'Words are the key to so many things. We seldom pass through the gate ourselves and we made a promise to always lock it behind us. But one of us . . .' She looked at Gorbo, who hung his head. 'Brightest and best of all Snergs, I do *not* think . . . one of us forgot.'

'I didn't forget the words,' said Gorbo, guiltily. 'I know the words:

I beg this gate to open wide,
I wish to be the other side.

No, wait . . .' His brow crinkled in concentration. 'That's wrong. That's what you say to *open* the gate. To shut it again, it's:

With this verse I turn the key,
Let no one now pass through this tree.

And then you spin around three times and touch your left ear with your right hand and your right foot with your left hand. Except,' confessed Gorbo, 'it's *just* possible that I touched my right ear with my left hand and my left foot with my right hand. If perhaps I was thinking about something else . . .'

'Or not thinking at all.' The Queen was stern. 'Brain like a string bag. You have caused a great deal of trouble, Gorbo.'

'Worse than that, the fellow's an assassin,' said King Kul. 'He is my prisoner, awaiting sentence for his crimes.'

'He didn't mean it. Please don't hurt him,' begged Pip.

'Not the centipedes,' implored Flora.

'Any attack upon a Royal Person, front or back, is treason and punishable by extreme unpleasantness,' declared the King. 'That is the law and there is no arguing with it, unless—'

'Unless what?' asked Pip and Flora and Queen Mercy, all at the same time.

'Unless he pays for his crime with his weight in gold,'

stated the King. 'That,' he added, eyeing Gorbo, 'would be quite a lot of gold.'

'Snergs do not deal in gold,' said Queen Mercy gravely. 'We find our treasures in starlight and rainbows and dewdrops on spiders' webs.'

'Pity,' said the King. 'Prepare the centipede pit!'

'Don't you have enough gold already?' wondered Pip, looking around him.

'Enough gold?' The King looked shocked. 'Never heard of such a thing. Nothing sings to the soul like the gleam of gold.'

'My father used to say the same about a glazed pie crust.' Gorbo's sigh made his chains rattle. 'He was a baker, you know. Nothing beats a good pie . . .'

'Pie . . .' There was some rapid conferring between the Snergs. Queen Mercy beckoned to Pompo and whispered into his ear. Squaring his shoulders, Pompo blew a blast on his horn.

'In return for the pitiful life of this pestiferous, pot-bellied, pigeon-witted prisoner . . .'

'Hey, steady on,' protested Gorbo.

'. . . Her Rotundiform Refulgence, Queen of the Snergs proposes a ransom of his weight in *pie*,' finished Pompo.

There was a silence. Then, 'What sort of pie?' asked the King.

'Any sort you like,' offered Queen Mercy. 'I have a most excellent and ingenious Head Pastry Fellow. He will bake it to your own specifications.'

'So much more useful than boring old gold,' said Flora encouragingly. 'Just think, you won't have to dust it.'

There were murmurings and much head-nodding among the courtiers, while the King sat frowning and tugging at the silver curls of his beard.

'Oh, very well,' he said at last. 'Proposal accepted. Release the Snerg.'

While Gorbo was being untwirled from his chains, the King dismissed his courtiers and his children and sat down to a second breakfast with the Expeditionary Force.

'We have important matters to discuss,' he announced. 'This witch and her ogre of a son must be dealt with. Kelps, Snergs and Noodles, it is time to put our differences aside.'

His eye fell on Pip and Flora. 'This is heavy business for young heads,' he said kindly. 'The Chancellor of the Money Bags will give you each a silver penny. Run along and buy yourselves a little something to take home with you.'

The market at Banrive was busy, full of Kelps bustling and jostling and shouting. The air smelt of onions and horse manure. Nobody paid any attention to two children and a dog.

'I hope they catch her – Malicia, Widow Meldrum, whatever she's called – before they send us back to Sunny Bay,' said Flora. 'Or we'll never know the end of the story.'

'All that stuff about the gate,' said Pip. 'Can you imagine Miss Watkyns doing that? Spinning in circles and touching her right ear with her left hand and her left foot with her right hand.'

'You're as bad as Gorbo,' Flora told him. 'It was the other way round. You touch your *left* ear with your *right* hand and your *right* foot with . . .' She broke off, laughing. Clutching at ears and feet, Pip was tying himself in knots. 'Not like that! Like this –' Flora stretched her arms out like a bird.

Around and around they both whirled, giddier and giddier, with Tiger yapping and dancing around their feet. At last, too dizzy to keep going, Pip collapsed and lay sprawled on his back with his eyes closed.

'Do you feel sick yet? You should be sicker than me,' he added, as Flora didn't answer. 'You ate more muffins than I did.'

Flora still didn't answer. Tiger's bark had a shrill, anxious note.

'Flora?' Pip opened his eyes. 'Hey – *Flora!*'

Flora had vanished.

CHAPTER 32

'What do you mean – *gone*?'

Kelps, Snergs, Captain Vanderdecken and his crew: they were all staring.

'I looked everywhere. She's disappeared.' Pip's breathing was ragged after his race back to the palace.

'The witch has taken her!' Gorbo flew up from his wooden stool. 'Oh, Gorbo – you floundering, flocculent flabber-wit!' He boxed his own ears, one side after the other. 'I should never have let you go out there! I knew she wasn't far away; she drove me here in the goat cart.'

The Queen sighed. 'Gorbo, did you not think to *say* so?'

'Fetch the gatekeeper!' ordered King Kul. 'He may have seen something.'

But the gatekeeper, when he arrived, was not much help.

'Plenty of traffic rolling in for the market,' he said. 'Not much going out. No lady drivers. One old man . . .'

'What did he look like?' demanded Queen Mercy.

The gatekeeper shrugged. 'Black cloak, black hat, black beard.'

'Can't have been her,' said King Kul. 'Not with a beard.'

'She's good at disguises,' warned Pip, remembering the warts and the chicken skin nose.

'Was the cart being pulled by a big black goat?' demanded Gorbo.

'Might have been,' said the gatekeeper. 'Might not. I can't be noticing everything. We get all sorts coming through. I had to cover my ears for the racket the fellow was making.'

'What racket?' asked King Kul.

'Bladder pipes,' said the man. 'Sounded like a herd of sick cows.'

'It *was* her – she must have had Flora hidden in the back of the cart!' Pip felt his stomach clench in a tight knot of dread. The pipes would have drowned out Flora's calls for help. 'Oh, hurry . . . please! We have to get her back!'

King Kul barked orders. Soldiers were dispatched at the gallop. One of them came back holding something black, ragged and hairy, loosely knotted together and smelling of goat.

'Mr Horniman's beard,' said Pip. 'She stole it from him.'

The Snergs were saddling up their ostriches. Captain Vanderdecken arranged his crew in marching order.

'Can't I come?' begged Pip.

Queen Mercy shook her head at him. 'I must keep at least one of you safe. Stay here with Gorbo. The Kelps will look after you. They are not the cruel race we thought them. All this time, we believed the stories. "They dine on babies boiled with rice" . . . Perhaps we should have come and found out the truth for ourselves.'

'I don't want to be safe and looked after,' said Pip, as he and Gorbo watched the last of the *Flying Dutchman's* crew tramp through the city gates. The ostriches and the

King's soldiers were already far ahead. 'Not when Flora's in danger . . .'

'They'll catch up with her soon enough.' Gorbo fingered his lucky acorn. Inside his shoes, he was crossing his toes.

'Only if they're going the right way,' said Pip. 'The witch won't stay at her cottage – she must know they'll come after her.'

'*Thief!*'

Pip and Gorbo both jumped as the shout rang out behind them. A large Kelp in charge of a fish stall was brandishing a long knife.

'If that beast comes near my fish again, I'll fillet him,' she threatened.

Crouched on the cobbles, crunching on a cod's head, was a black cat with a crooked tail and only one eye. Pip caught hold of Tiger just in time.

'Gorbo – look! It's Gubbins. He must have followed us here. He's been tracking Flora since we left Sunny Bay – he was behind us the whole time. At least, I think he was behind us . . .' Pip frowned. Now he thought about it, who had been following whom? Might it have been Gubbins that Tiger was chasing all along? Whichever way around it was, he hadn't forgotten the witch's words. 'Gubbins has a nose like a shark scenting blood . . .'

'We don't want any sharks,' said Gorbo definitely. 'Or blood. We just want Miss Flora.'

'Yes,' agreed Pip. 'And Gubbins is going to find her for us!'

In their excitement, Pip and Gorbo joined hands and swung each other around in the traditional Snerg greeting, knocking into the fishwife and upsetting a tray of sprats.

'Hoodlum dumplings,' she complained. 'I don't know why the King hasn't chopped your heads off by now.'

'Because, dear madam, he is not the Bad Man that we thought he was,' Gorbo told her. 'It turns out that it was all a mistake: Kelps and Snergs are now very good friends.'

'Speak for yourself,' sniffed the woman. 'I hope you can pay for those fish.'

'It's not as if we want them,' grumbled Pip, reluctantly handing over his penny.

'Yes, we do,' said Gorbo. 'Lend me that hat of yours.' Pushing Tiger's nose out of the way, he scooped fish into

Pip's velvet hat. 'Here, puss.'

Gubbins had finished his cod's head. He stood up, stretched and sauntered over, whiskers twitching in the fishy air.

'If you want any more, you're going to have to earn it,' Gorbo told him, dangling a sprat just out of his reach. 'Go on, puss. Show us the way.'

In which Malicia climbs to Goblin Crag and Golithos has a bad day. Gorbo is a hero after all, Pip pulls off the perfect catch, Flora says what she thinks and Tiger plays his part.

CHAPTER 33

'W'here are we going, Muzzer?'

'Underground, my son,' said Widow Meldrum. 'Where we won't be found. There's a way in through the rock, up there between those crags.' She pointed to the top of the slope they were climbing. 'A goblin door. It leads deep inside the hill. They can search, if they want to, for a hundred years; they'll never find us.'

'I don't like underground,' said Golithos dolefully. 'Underground is for small people. It bumps my head.'

'With luck, it will bump some sense into you.' The witch prodded Flora with the end of her umbrella. 'Don't dawdle, girl – get a move on!'

Flora, for the hundredth time, had tripped over her embroidered skirt, its hem now dusty and fraying. It is not easy climbing a steep hill in a long dress with your hands roped together. Her thin satin shoes, borrowed from a Kelp princess with smaller feet, had worn through.

She had left Banrive bouncing in the back of the goat cart, tied in a large sack, with the sound of the bladder pipes drowning her shouts for help. It was a relief when the bumping stopped and the sack was untied. It was less cheering to find herself back at the witch's cottage, with Golithos's big moon face peering down at her, especially when he started licking his lips.

'Stop dribbling!' his mother had commanded him. 'And help me load the cart.'

They had soon set off again, the cart piled high with pots and pans, sticks of furniture, the toad in his wicker cage, several baskets of caterwauling cats, a great many pairs of purple stockings, a large lilac hat and the remains of a gingerbread house.

Golithos led the goat, trying to keep out of reach of his

horns: Mr Horniman was still sulking at the theft of his beard. Flora had a rope around her wrists and another around her middle. Widow Meldrum held the end of it, poking Flora on with the spike of her umbrella.

The hill grew steeper. They were following the course of a riverbed, long since dried up. Down on the plain, Banrive's battlements looked very small and far away.

'Can't we rest, Muzzer?' Golithos was fretful. 'The sun is too bright. It makes me dizzy. And you're making the girl walk too fast. She'll get thin and stringy. She's already look-ing less juicy.'

'So what? She's not for eating,' retorted the witch. 'How many times do I have to tell you?'

Golithos sighed. 'Then what *is* she for?'

'Yes, what?' said Flora, sounding braver than she felt. 'You don't want me cluttering up your nice cave. I'll only get in the way. I'd leave me behind, if I were you.'

Widow Meldrum laughed. 'No, no – you're mine now. I knew you were the right one, as soon as I saw you. I saw it in your eyes. Not quite like other girls. Sulky. Angry with people, angry with life. Just like I was, at your age. We are the same, you and I.'

'We're not,' said Flora.

'They'd only take you back to that orphanage,' said the witch. 'All those rules, and manners, and doing as you're told. How can you be happy there? I made a promise, long ago, that I would destroy that place. I keep my promises. Soon it will crumble like gingerbread – there will be nothing left but a heap of ashes.'

'You won't do it,' said Flora. 'Miss Watkyns won't let you.'

'She is making it difficult,' admitted the witch. 'My goody-goody little sister has ringed the place around with her charms. I can't get past them – but you can. When you are ready – when your mind and mine have become one – you will go back to Sunny Bay. Miss Watkyns won't turn her lost lamb away; how could she? She will take you in and when the time is right – yours will be the hand that lights the match. You will be my instrument and do what I cannot. Wouldn't you like to see it all go up in smoke? Think of the flames, so bright and beautiful, burning away all that dreariness and unhappiness.'

'No,' said Flora.

'And afterwards, when there is nothing left,' said Malicia dreamily, 'Felicia Watkyns will be gone. She will have disappeared.'

Flora stopped walking. 'What are you going to do to her?'

'Muzzer will turn Auntie Watkyns into a toad, like Mr Bunphatt,' said Golithos. 'And we shall have a new pet.'

'Whatever gave you that idea?' said the witch. 'Turn my own sister into a toad? I am not so unfeeling. Not a toad. Something prettier. Have you ever seen a fire salamander?'

Flora shook her head, fiercely enough to make her hair fly. 'I won't do it! The orphanage isn't like it used to be. They are kind to us. Nobody beats us. There are picnics and games and . . . and custard.'

'Custard?' sneered the witch. 'Is that all it takes to make you happy? Aren't you worth more than that? Miss Watkyns doesn't care about you – any more than she cared about me, her sister. I begged her to come with me when I left Sunny Bay. She refused, leaving me to set out into the wide world with only a toad for company. Is that fair?'

'You'd set the orphanage on fire,' Flora pointed out. 'She

stayed to rescue the other children. Nobody made you run away.'

'You don't know what it was like.' Malicia cast a glance full of hatred at the toad in his cage. 'Adolphus Bunphatt,' she said bitterly. 'The sort of bloated pudding-bag who carves himself a roast dinner while starving children slurp watered gruel. Before every crust of bread, we had to stand up and thank him. A sneeze, a dropped spoon, a whispered word – and we were caned. If we cried, he beat us harder. He is paying for it now – he has to beg me for his worms. That is half my promise kept – but only half. Burn down the orphanage for me, Flora, and I will care for you like my own daughter. Look, here is a pretty present to prove it – see.'

Malicia held out her hand. On her palm lay half of a little silver heart – tarnished and green for lack of polish – on a string of coral beads.

'Put it on,' coaxed the witch, fastening it around Flora's neck.

'Too tight,' protested Flora. 'It's strangling me.'

'Stop complaining,' said Malicia sharply. 'You had better

learn to do as you're told without making such a fuss, now that you belong to me.'

'I don't belong to you,' said Flora fiercely. 'I belong at Sunny Bay, with Pip and Tiger. Miss Watkyns grew up in the orphanage with Mr Bunphatt too, but she's tried to make things better. You just want to make everything worse! And Miss Watkyns *does* care about us. She sent Queen Mercy and Captain Vanderdecken to look for us.'

'Ah, the gallant rescue party,' taunted Malicia. Handing the end of Flora's rope to Golithos, she lifted her skull bowl down from the cart. 'Old men and a handful of Snergs. King Kul is entertaining them in his banqueting hall. Show a Snerg a feast and he'd forget his own grandmother. Have they even realized that you're missing, I wonder?'

'Pip has,' said Flora firmly. 'He and Gorbo will come for me.'

The witch gave a crack of laughter. 'Gorbo? That one couldn't rescue a lettuce from a snail!' Settling herself on a nearby boulder with the skull on her lap, she passed her hand over the nightshade jelly and peered into its depths.

'Oh dear,' she mocked. 'I see ostriches, flapping in circles, their riders not knowing which way to go; I see confused old men marching in opposite directions. I see soldiers searching an empty cottage. Poor little Flora . . . I'm afraid that it is the goblin caves for you, after all. A few weeks down there in the dark and you'll be ready to do as I say.'

Perhaps Malicia should have looked harder. What she had *not* seen in the jelly were two small figures and a dog – all of them chasing a one-eyed cat.

CHAPTER 34

Miss Watkyns sat at her desk, her chin cupped in one hand, twisting a lock of dark hair around her finger. She was watching her goldfish. Left flick of the tail, dart to the right, up to the surface, quick turn, dive! Over and over and over again.

'No,' said Miss Watkyns abruptly, pushing back her chair. 'It won't do! Heinrich Cornelius, you need a bigger bowl.'

As she set off down the corridor, a small boy, late for his Latin, came hurtling around the corner. Seeing her, he skidded to a guilty halt.

'William,' said Miss Watkyns. 'Do you see that sign on

the wall? What does it say?'

William hung his head. '*No Running in the Corridors,* Miss Watkyns.'

'So it does,' agreed Miss Watkyns. 'I want you to ignore that sign.' Pulling it off the wall, she scrumpled it into a ball. 'Run faster, William. Run as fast as you can. What are you waiting for? Go, go, go!'

She flapped her hands. William took off like a startled hare.

'Yes,' said Miss Watkyns to the empty corridor. 'I have stifled these children, hedging them in with rules and rosemary. I was only trying to keep them safe, but I have been too rigid. It's never too late to learn from our mistakes. Sometimes rules must be bent, risks must be taken – life, after all, must be lived. From now on, things at Sunny Bay are going to be different . . .'

CHAPTER 35

The sun beat down, high and hot. The climbers had paused for a rest. Golithos lay snoring in the shade of a pine tree, a handkerchief over his face. To stop them yowling, the cats had been allowed out of their baskets to sprawl in the heat. Mr Horniman, freed from the cart shafts, nibbled at a thornbush. Mr Bunphatt sheltered beneath Malicia's umbrella while she sat stooped over her jelly. It showed her what she most wanted to see: the Sunny Bay Home for Superfluous and Accidentally Parentless Children crackling and burning. The sound of the flames was her lullaby; her head began to droop.

The end of Flora's rope was knotted around a pine branch, out of her reach. She was wide awake. *Pip, where are you . . .?*

A long, long way down the hill, something moved.

Two dots and a white speck, following a black speck. Eyes fixed, Flora held her breath. Hope bubbled up inside her. *Hurry*, she urged the dots; *please, please, come quickly.* They were too far away. Malicia would wake up and march Flora underground before they could reach her. She would be lost for ever and never see Pip or Gorbo or Tiger again . . .

Time. They need more time. She looked down at her roped wrists. Then at the ends of Golithos's bootlaces . . .

What a good thing, thought Flora, *that I sat next to Wilmus at the Queen's feast. And that he taught me how to tie an Un-untieable knot . . .*

It wasn't easy with her hands roped together but a few minutes later, after a lot of frowning and looping and threading and tugging, she pulled the bootlaces tight and sat back. *That should slow us down a bit*, she thought. *But not enough.* The dots on the hillside did not seem to have grown much larger. The witch stirred and muttered. Any minute now, she would wake. Flora's hope began to fizzle away.

Mr Horniman had torn all the leaves off his thornbush and was looking for something else to do. Lowering his horns, he tried head-butting a passing bee, then he went up on his hind legs to investigate the contents of the cart.

There aren't many things a goat won't eat. They will certainly eat gingerbread.

Help yourself, Mr Horniman, Flora willed him on. *Eat as much as you like.*

After finishing off the roof and top floor of the gingerbread house, the goat began to look a little doubtful. Sitting back on his haunches he uttered one surprised bleat, then keeled over.

The bleat woke Malicia. Glancing up at the angle of the sun, she frowned and threw a pebble at Golithos.

'Up you get, Slouchworm. It's time we were underground.'

She reached for the skull bowl again. Flora froze. If she saw those two black dots in the jelly, then what? There would probably be two more frogs hopping in the dry riverbed while she, Flora, would be swallowed up by the hill.

Golithos sat up, rubbing his eyes and yawning.

His mother threw another pebble at him. 'Hurry up. Untie the girl and get that goat back in harness.'

Golithos stood up. He tried to take a step, but his knotted laces wouldn't let him. He tottered, arms flailing, then toppled forwards. There was a *thud*, as skull met skull. Golithos had landed face first in the jelly.

'Numbskull!' raged his mother. 'Look what you've done!'

'Blood! Bleeding!' wailed the ogre, clutching his forehead.

Pushing him out of the way, the witch scooped up the shimmering purple blobs. Dropping them back into the bowl, she tried to smooth the surface – but it was no use. Nothing stirred in its depths, nothing showed itself to her: it was just a bowl of broken jelly.

Golithos had discovered his laces.

'It was *her*!' he snivelled, pointing at Flora. 'I don't like her, Muzzer. She isn't kind.'

Malicia raged at them both, still bent over her jelly fragments, while Golithos struggled with the Un-untieable knot. Flora wasn't listening; she was gazing downhill. The figures were clearly visible now – too visible. Somehow, she had to send a warning. What was it Gorbo had taught them when they met him in the wood, before the wobsers came swarming? Cupping her hands to her mouth, Flora made the call of the discombobulated cuckoo.

Oo-k-uck . . . ooo-k-uck . . .

Would they hear? Flora saw the figures halt. One of them turned to face the other; an arm pointed up the hill and then they were gone, slipping between the trees.

'There's something wrong with the girl, Muzzer. She's making noises.' Golithos was staring at her. 'She's got hairballs.'

'I swallowed a fly,' lied Flora, doing some pretend coughing. 'I think it's stuck in my throat.'

'Are you still fiddling with those laces?' snapped Malicia, frowning at her son. 'Anyone whose head wasn't full of stone dust would just take those shoes *off.*'

It was then that she noticed Mr Horniman.

'Why did you give him so much rope?' she stormed at Golithos. 'Now look at him – no use to anyone! Put him in the cart. You'll have to pull it yourself.'

'I can't walk any further,' said Flora piteously. 'My feet hurt. I've got blisters . . .'

'Useless girl!' Malicia folded her umbrella with a snap. Sparks flew. 'Put her in the cart too, or she'll hold us up.'

Tugging off his shoes, Golithos picked Flora up and tipped her, not too gently, in among the pots and pans and wooden stools.

He stood over her with Mr Horniman draped across his shoulders. 'Budge up, Unkind Girl.'

Flora shuffled backwards, wincing as she sat on the bladder pipes. And that was when it happened. Goatless, the cart had been resting with its shafts on the ground. It was heavily laden, on a steep slope. Now, as the weight shifted to the back, the shafts swung up and the wheels began to slip.

'Hey!' Feeling it jolt beneath her, Flora grabbed hold of the side. 'Hey, be careful – it's going to—'

But the wheels were turning now, picking up speed. Golithos lunged, clutching at a shaft, but he was hampered by the goat on his shoulders and lost his grip.

'What are you *doing*?' shrieked his mother. 'You block-headed, clod-hopping lump! You sedimentary slobber-mouth! Megalithic mongrel! I should have given you to the goblins to play with when you were born. I should have left you out for the eagles. I should have dropped you into a canyon. I should have . . .'

Whatever came next, Flora didn't hear it. The cart was racketing and bouncing down the riverbed, stones skittering and spraying out beneath the wheels. All she could do was hang on to the sides, wondering what would happen when they reached the bottom and how much it was going to hurt.

CHAPTER 36

'What's that noise?' asked Pip, tilting his head to listen. They had stopped to catch their breath between the trees. The black cat had led them uphill at a smart pace with Tiger on his tail, panting and straining at his string, towing Pip behind him. Gorbo looked up at the clear blue sky and scratched his head. The cat curled around his legs; there was one sprat left in the velvet hat. 'Can't be thunder . . .'

'Gorbo . . .' Pip was staring uphill. 'Gorbo – *look*!'

The answer was rumbling into view: the goatless cart came bucketing down towards them, spewing out the witch's possessions left and right. A figure clung to the side of the cart, sunlight glinting on her fair hair.

'Flora . . .' Pip felt a cold rush of horror.

'Don't you worry, Master Pip,' said Gorbo, starting to scramble down the riverbank. 'It may be a bit messy, and Miss Flora may get a few bruises, but I'll stop that cart if it's the last thing I do. And if it *is* . . . you can have all my string. Remember me to Aunt Flumper. Look after young Tiger. And tell the Queen, Gorbo did his best.'

'You can't let that cart crash straight into you!' protested Pip. 'You'll be . . . Gorbo, *no*! I won't let you. Here, take Tiger. I know what to do, but we don't have much time.'

The trees grew close to the bank here, stretching their branches out over the empty riverbed. Pip cast a glance up at the cart – much closer now – then at the branches, measuring height and distance. A moment later he was up off the ground and into a tree, climbing like the circus child that he had once been. Crawling out along his chosen branch, he felt his heart hammering and the familiar fizzing in his veins. In the old days, the fizz had been terror – not of falling, but of what his father would do to him if he made a mistake. If he was afraid now, it was the fear of something happening to Flora. Without his father's eye on him, making him clumsy and stupid, he could do this; he knew he could.

He let himself drop, fingers gripping bark. Would the branch hold? He hoped so. The cart was very close now. Would Flora know what he needed her to do? Yes – Flora always knew; she didn't need words. As long as she saw him in time.

Swing. Use your legs. Pull up. Hook your knees over. Hang down. Swing.

There was the cart – and there was Flora, pale face, hair flying. She had seen him; she was on her feet – unsteady, catching the side of the cart to keep her balance.

Don't wobble, Flora. Stand tall. Reach for me . . .

She understood. Bracing herself, she reached up her tied hands . . . and Pip caught her.

The three of them stood on the bank, watching the cart go on its way. Down and down until, near the bottom of the hill, it met a bend in the riverbed and smashed into the bank. There was a splintering of wood; what was left of

Widow Meldrum's belongings erupted into the air, then came raining down again. The wreckage of the cart lay on its side, one wheel still turning.

'What if I'd still been in it?' Flora was trembling. 'What if you hadn't come?'

'Of course we came,' said Pip.

'*What ifs* don't count,' declared Gorbo, untying Flora's hands. 'This is quite nice rope, actually – do you mind if I keep it? What matters is *What is*. And right now, we are back together again – the three of us.'

'Um . . . about to be four,' said Pip, pointing. 'Look.' Golithos was lolloping towards them, arms waving to keep his balance as he thundered down the hill.

'If I only had my bow and arrows,' lamented Gorbo. 'I'd stick him as full of needles as a portly-pine but . . . no, wait . . . let me see . . .it's just possible . . . I *think*,' said Gorbo, sounding very much surprised, 'that I might be having an idea.' Shrugging his string bag off his shoulder, he began unravelling it. 'Here.' He handed the loose end to Flora. 'Loop it around that tree – about so high – and both of you hang on tight. *Don't let go.*' And letting the remains of the bag unravel as he went, Gorbo was gone – skipping across the riverbed towards the trees on the other side.

Golithos came pounding downhill, red-faced and snarling.

'Where is she? Unkind Girl. Muzzer wants her back. Muzzer's very angry – more angry if I don't catch her. And fetch bladder pipes and best cauldron and pickled heart and purple-y hat, but most of all Girl.'

Eyes ahead, scanning the hillside for Flora, he was not looking where he was going. The string, stretched across the riverbed, caught him on the shins. He rocked, he swayed, he bellowed – and crashed to the ground.

'Oh dear,' sighed Flora. 'That's twice in one day. Poor old Golithos.'

Hooves thudded. There were shouts. Around the side of the hill came galloping soldiers, several ostriches and, gallantly keeping up the rear, the crew of the *Flying Dutchman* with muskets at the ready.

'You're a bit late,' Pip told them. 'We've already rescued Flora.'

'Out of my way.' Sir Percival drew his sword. 'I shall slay

this ogre.'

'Actually, no,' said Flora. 'You won't.' As she knelt beside Golithos, he turned his face towards her. She had a moment of doubt, seeing his once-upon-a-time child-eating teeth so near, but his nose was bleeding and there were tears in his eyes.

'I'm sorry,' she told him. 'I'm sorry that I tied your laces together. I'm sorry that I made your mother shout at you. I'm sorry that I've made you fall over again. Just lie quietly and don't do anything silly, and there won't be any slaying.' She looked sternly at Sir Percival. 'He's had a lot to put up with, you know, having that witch as his mother. Parents,' declared Flora, 'should *not* be unkind to their children – not if they want them to turn out right. It's hard to grow up good and charming and clever if people who ought to know better make you feel the opposite inside.'

If Flora was thinking of her own mother, with her pearls and parties and perfectly powdered nose, Pip was remembering his father, swollen and bristling with rage, always shouting, always the same words: *useless . . . stupid . . . no-good waste of space . . .*

'She's right, you know,' said Pip.

'King's orders,' insisted Sir Percival. 'The brute's a man-eater.'

'Not any more,' said Flora firmly. 'Everybody makes mistakes. We can all change.'

'Very true,' said Queen Mercy. 'Spoken like a Snerg.'

'Fellow deserves a second chance,' agreed Captain Vanderdecken. 'Strapping lad – make a fine tuba player.'

'We'll take him back to Sunny Bay,' decided Flora. 'Miss Watkyns will know what to do with him.'

A quiver ran through Golithos. 'Not Watkyns,' he whimpered. 'Wicked Watkyns – she'll hurt me. Tweaks and twinges and all my biters rattling around in my head. She'll make them all fall out – then I shall *never* be able to crunch up children again.'

'Could you try not to talk about eating children just now?' suggested Flora, in his ear. 'It isn't helping. There are a lot of other foods that taste much better, I should think – you've just never tried them.'

But Golithos was still trembling. 'Wickedy wickedy Watkyns,' he repeated. 'Nasty. Muzzer said so. Muzzer knows best.'

'Mothers don't always know best,' said Flora. 'And you shouldn't always believe what you're told. Sometimes you need to find things out yourself. Look at this lot.' She waved a hand at the gathered soldiers and Snergs. 'They've been believing stories about each other for years and years and it all turned out to be nonsense. I'm afraid we are going to have to tie you up,' she added apologetically. 'Just for a little while. As for you,' she told Sir Percival, 'do stop waving your sword about. Can't you see it's disgruntling the ostriches? Hadn't you better go after the witch? She's heading for those crags.' Flora pointed up the hill. 'Once she gets there, she's going underground. Rather you than me, if you have to tell King Kul you've lost her for a second time.'

CHAPTER 37

A little-known fact about goblins is their fondness for home improvement. In the summer months, when the days are long and bright and goblins are stuck underground for long hours at a time, they occupy themselves with plans for interior design. An extension here; some demolition there. They knock through walls and build tasteful arches. They swap the stalactites and stalagmites around. They redirect the plumbing of their underground streams. And they move the doors – usually when they're expecting visitors.

Malicia should have thought of this. She had not.

She climbed the hill at a brisk pace. She was travelling light, with only her umbrella and six black cats, all on leads of purple ribbon. She had seen the cart crash, she had seen the felling of Golithos and she had seen the glint of armour riding around the hill. She knew she was pursued.

'They are too slow, too stupid,' she told the cats. 'They won't catch us.'

But when she reached the top, the goblin doorway wasn't there.

She rapped with the handle of her umbrella, putting her ear to the stone. She could hear gibbering and giggling and pattering feet on the other side, but there was no way in. Behind her, the sounds of hooves and feet and voices were much closer now. The cats mewled, tangling their ribbons. Rathbones, Grimalkin, Pyewacket, Hodge, Sister Gutspill, Vinegar Tom . . . One missing, as usual.

Beyond the crags lay the sea, sparkling in the sunlight. 'It isn't the end,' said Malicia. 'Not yet.'

'We're too late,' said Pip, as the band of witch-hunters reached the summit. 'She's gone.'

'Enemy above,' announced Captain Vanderdecken, peering upwards through his telescope.

Malicia had climbed to the top of a tall column of rock. She stood there in her gown of grape-dark silk, her blackberry hair swirling around her. Her umbrella was in her hand; her cats mewed at her feet.

Sir Percival cleared his throat. 'I, Sir Percival the Pugnacious, charge you Malicia Watkyns . . .'

'My name is Meldrum,' she interrupted him. 'I am a respectable widow.'

'Only because she left her husband out in the sun,' murmured Pip.

Sir Percival kicked his horse forward. 'You are charged with Kidnap, Gratuitous Amphibious Metamorphosis . . .'

'What?' said Gorbo.

'I think he means turning people into frogs,' said Flora.

'. . . and Being Generally Villainous,' went on Sir Percival. 'I am to deliver you to Banrive on the King's orders.'

Malicia laughed. 'Thank the King for his kind invitation – but I would prefer not to spend the rest of my days in his dungeon.'

'You can't stay up there for ever, Malicia,' said Queen Mercy. 'I am sorry it has to end like this but if you spend your life causing trouble, it is going to catch up with you in the end.'

'Pompo, rather out of breath, blew a blast on his horn. 'By order of Their Joint, Judicious and (Generally) Jocular Majesties, Queen Mercy of the Snergs and King Kul of the Kelps—'

'Seize her!' ordered Sir Percival.

Two Kelp soldiers obediently dismounted from their horses and began to climb the rock. Malicia laughed. Gathering the cats' ribbons into one hand, she raised her other arm.

Pip felt a stab of dread – he knew, suddenly, what was in the witch's mind.

'The umbrella!' he shouted. 'She's going to turn us all into . . .'

Was Pip right? Who knows how many little frogs might have hopped down the hillside that day if Tiger, straining and baying at the end of his string, had not at that moment pulled free. The sight of his enemies – six of them growling and hissing at him – was too much. He sprang forward, the end of his lead slipping through Flora's fingers, and threw himself at the rock.

The witch's cats pulled at their ribbons, yowling and lashing their tails. As they tangled around her legs, Malicia kicked out at them – and lost her balance.

The watchers below drew in their breath in one gasp. Malicia teetered, floundering on the narrow ledge as she tried to right herself, then toppled . . . and was gone – surely to be dashed to pieces on the rocks below.

Or not.

Her laugh came back to them, thin and high like the shriek of a gull.

'Enemy flying south-south-west,' reported the Captain, tilting his telescope.

There, seated side-saddle upon her umbrella. Malicia was riding the waves of the wind. As she shook out their ribbons, her cats bounded forward through thin air, bearing her aloft as they headed out to sea.

The Captain shook his head. 'In all my time, I've never seen anything like *that.*'

'Perhaps it is for the best,' said Queen Mercy. 'If she is

gone from these lands, she cannot harm us.'

'Maybe not,' said Gorbo, 'but it seems to me that she'll very likely go and bother some other poor folk who've done nothing to deserve it.'

Queen Mercy blinked at him. 'That,' she said, 'was a surprisingly sensible remark. Something has happened to you, Gorbo. I do believe you're actually *thinking*.'

Pip and Flora were watching the witch. She was following the coast, where the water had nibbled at the land to form little bays. Pip's eyes lingered on one of those bays, a horseshoe of golden sand between two promontories. Perched on the cliffs above it was a big stone house with tall chimneys. A house that looked oddly familiar.

'Captain, may I borrow your telescope?'

'Ay, lad.' The Captain passed it to him. 'Can you see pirates?'

'No,' said Pip, putting it to his eye, 'but . . . Flora, look!' He handed her the telescope. 'Over there. It's Sunny Bay!'

'Well I'll be jiggered, so it is!' said the Captain. He took out his pocket watch and frowned. 'What's keeping Mr Halibut and Mr Pollock? Two minutes past the hour – and

I'd like to know why they haven't fired Doris!'

It was just as the distant shape of the witch floated into the bay that it came: the flash of light; the reverberating boom of the cannon – Dead Men Doris making her noon salute. The gulls rose up in a screeching cloud, as they always did, before sinking back down on to the waves. Drifting among them were shreds of silk and the tattered remains of a purple umbrella . . .

For a second time, the watchers on the crags stood in shocked silence. It was Flora, holding the telescope to her eye, who broke it.

'What's that?'

A speck of black had separated itself from the gulls and was fluttering upwards.

Captain Vanderdecken took the telescope from her and peered through it. 'Nothing out there but gulls.'

As they turned to go back down the hill, Flora hoped he was right. *Because if you ask me*, she thought, *that speck looked a lot like a bat.* And who had ever heard of a bat flying out to sea?

She didn't say it out loud. After all, she'd had plenty of practice in keeping things to herself. *And what's the point,* thought Flora, *of spoiling a nice happy ending?*

In which Pip and Flora are back at Sunny Bay, where all is not exactly the same as before. Miss Watkyns takes in a new — and surprisingly large — Accidentally Parentless Orphan, Tiger eats an invitation and there is a whiff of cinnamon in the air . . .

CHAPTER 38

Miss Watkyns sat at her desk, very upright, hair neatly pinned. Behind her, the open window let in the sea-salty sunshine and the shriek of the gulls. On the bench opposite her, a thin, dark-eyed boy sat swinging his legs. He sat there alone.

Two weeks had passed since Pip and Flora had returned to Sunny Bay; their adventures were already beginning to seem a distant memory.

They had parted with the Kelps on excellent terms (except, perhaps, with Sir Percival). King Kul had provided them with an armed guard across the Troll Bridge, in case of trouble, but the Troll had not raised her hairy head. (She heard the trip-trapping of so many feet above her head and regretted the waste, but she had eaten a large crocopotamus the evening before and was still suffering from indigestion.)

Avoiding the Twisted Trees, they were soon back at the town of the Snergs. Here, the sight of Golithos had caused some alarm until Queen Mercy gave her word that he was no longer *fierce of fang*.

'He is still rather *foul of breath*,' admitted Flora, privately to Pip, 'but it would be very unkind to mention it – and I'm sure Miss Watkyns will find him a toothbrush.'

Snergs have forgiving hearts. As soon as they grasped that the ogre meant no harm, they welcomed him – plying him with cake and kindness until he was quite overcome and an extra-large handkerchief had to be found to mop up the fall of his tears.

The children left the town of the Snergs riding on cinnamon bears, flanked by ostrich outriders. They had, understandably, had hopes of parading like this up the orphanage's gravel drive, admired and envied by all the other orphans, but in this they were disappointed. Miss

Watkyns, forewarned of their arrival, had made rapid arrangements for the others to be down on the beach with Mr Gribblestone, to enjoy a lecture on the subject of geological rock formations.

Comfortable as it was to hear the cry of the gulls and breathe in the familiar scents of rosemary, lavender and sea salt, both Pip and Flora could feel nervous wings flapping inside them. It seemed a very long time since they had disrupted Captain Vanderdecken's band practice. They had already, without being asked, apologized to the Captain and crew.

'Worse things happen at sea,' the Captain had said cheerfully, and hands had been shaken all round.

But they still had to face Miss Watkyns.

She had been there, tall and straight, to greet them at the orphanage door. After one quick, noticing look at their faces, as they slid off their cinnamon bears, she said calmly that she was glad to see them back again. Beside her, Miss Scadging gazed up at Golithos.

'Oh dear,' she said. 'Oh dear, oh dear. He has outgrown himself, poor fellow. I must speak to Cook. We are going to need a *great* deal of custard.'

The children were sent to the kitchen for milk and biscuits.

'And the same for him,' added Miss Watkyns, with a glance at Tiger.

Pip and Flora hadn't seen her again that day. Nor the next. Along with the bears and the ostriches, Miss Watkyns had disappeared.

'She's gone on a visit,' said Miss Scadging casually – as if such a thing had ever happened before. 'She'll be back soon.'

'She's gone to find out exactly what happened,' guessed Pip. 'And Malicia was her sister, after all. Do you suppose she minds about her . . . going?'

Flora shrugged. She hadn't forgotten what she had seen through the Captain's telescope. Should she tell? Miss Watkyns had never heard her speak. It seemed a big leap, to go from months of silence to: *I think your sister may have turned into a bat.*

And now, quietly and without any fuss, Miss Watkyns had come back. Pip, struggling to make sense of his times tables in Mr Gribblestone's arithmetic class, had seen her walking up the drive. With one hand she led a big black goat; from the other swung a wicker basket containing a large toad. Mr Bunphatt too had come back to Sunny Bay.

Pip had been working hard at his lessons in the days since his return. If he ever came face to face with another wobser, he wouldn't need Flora there to rescue him: he could do his own arithmetic now. And as nobody knows – not for sure – when they might need to read the signs on a witch's cottage, he had been studious with his reading too.

'You'd think he was a different boy,' Mr Gribblestone had remarked to Miss Scadging.

'And Flora's found her voice again,' said Miss Scadging. 'It just goes to show that you should never, ever give up on a child.' Mindful of Miss Watkyns's instructions, she was keeping an eye on Golithos. Sunny Bay's newest orphan had caused a few problems – there was no furniture to fit him, let alone clothes, and he got through six gallons of custard a day. Now he was out in the garden, sitting in the grass with a daisy chain in his tendrils of hair. Some of the smaller girls were teaching him clapping games – and he was hardly dribbling at all. 'It's true,' decided Miss Scadging. 'We can all change.'

But this morning, at the sight of Miss Watkyns, Pip's sums had gone wobbly. Arithmetic was followed by geography and Mr Gribblestone was pointing at him, wanting to know the capital of Belgium.

'Um,' said Pip. 'Er . . .'

Mr Gribblestone sighed – and it was at that moment that the message arrived. Miss Watkyns wished to see Pip.

Feeling the empty space beside him, Pip wished it contained Flora. The girls were outside playing cricket. Miss Scadging, with Miss Watkyns's blessing, had made certain changes to their timetable. There was a good deal less embroidery and a good deal more woodwork, inventing and elementary chicken-keeping. The boys were all learning to knit, and the best way of roasting potatoes.

Pip heard the whoops and cheers as someone hit a six. He could hear Flora's voice, raised with the others. The other girls used to leave Flora alone, finding her silence strange. Now they coaxed her away to join in their games.

He hadn't quite got used to that, not yet.

Underneath a small table, where the sun was not too bright, Mr Bunphatt crouched, golden-eyed, in his basket.

'Will you turn him back again?' Pip blurted it out, then wished that he hadn't.

'The creature will be released in a damp, dark spot,' said Miss Watkyns calmly. 'With plenty of worms.' She stretched out a hand to stroke the black cat curled at her elbow.

There were, suddenly, an unexpected number of black cats in Sunny Bay. They had arrived out of the blue – much to the surprise of the fisherman whose boat they had landed on in a yowling, spitting, tail-lashing heap, all trailing a frayed length of purple ribbon.

'Fell right out of the sky,' he told anyone who'd listen. 'Raining cats, it was.'

Back on dry land, the cats had distributed themselves around the bay – one with the butcher, one with the baker, one with the blacksmith and one at the Lobster Pot Inn. Two remained with the fisherman and his wife. When a seventh cat arrived with Pip and Flora – a cat with a crooked tail and one green eye – Miss Watkyns surprised everybody by opening the door to it and making it welcome.

Watching Gubbins rub his cheek against Miss Watkyns's hand, Pip noticed that something was missing.

'The fish,' said Pip. 'Where's it gone?'

'Into the pond,' Miss Watkyns told him. 'Heinrich Cornelius needed a more interesting life. You told me that yourself. I owe you an apology, Pip.'

Pip blinked and wriggled on his bench. What was the matter with Miss Watkyns?

'I told you that certain things didn't exist,' she went on, 'I let you think that they were just make-believe . . .'

'Wobsers,' said Pip. 'And witches . . .' Should he tell her that he knew her secret? 'You knew all along that they were real.'

'I'm sorry,' admitted Miss Watkyns. 'I wanted to keep you safe. I thought that what you didn't know about – what you didn't believe in – couldn't harm you. I was wrong. You can't keep things locked away and pretend they're not there. You must face up to them, with a brave heart. You have taught me that – you and Flora and Gorbo. Just as you taught the Snergs and the Kelps that they should get to know their neighbours before believing bad things of them. All this is worth more than knowing the capital of Belgium. You may tell Mr Gribblestone that I said so.'

'Oh . . .' Pip felt himself flush. He was wondering whether to ask her if she wouldn't mind telling Mr Gribblestone that herself, when a cricket ball hurtled in through the open window. It missed Miss Watkyns's head by a hair's breadth, disturbing the cat and landing with a *thwunk!* at Pip's feet.

'Oh, *Golithos!*' cried several different voices at once.

Miss Watkyns gave a sigh. 'Golithos . . .' she murmured. 'Of course.'

With his long arms and legs, the ogre was a useful player once he had got the hang of the rules; everybody wanted him on their team.

'Is this really the best place for him?' wondered Miss Watkyns. 'So many children . . .'

'It's all right,' said Pip. 'You don't have to worry. He's forgotten all about eating children since he discovered custard.'

Pip bent to pick up the cricket ball – and froze. It was

moving by itself. Swerving politely past his feet, it rose in the air, hovered for a moment, then shot back out through the window to land with a *thwack!* on Golithos's bat. Pip looked at Miss Watkyns. She sat very still and composed, stroking the black cat. He opened his mouth, then shut it again. Some moments are better left silent – words just get in the way.

Pushing back her chair, Miss Watkyns crossed to the window and looked down at the cricketers, who had gone rather quiet since the return of their ball.

'Flora,' she called, 'would you come up here, please. I have something to say to you.'

Flushed and breathless, Flora arrived with Tiger at her heels. The puppy took one look at the cat and hurled himself at the desk in a flurry of fur and fury. Miss Watkyns raised her eyebrows at him and he flopped to the floor with his tail between his legs.

'We do not have many rules here at Sunny Bay,' Miss Watkyns informed him, 'but some must remain. Good manners towards cats at all times is one of them. Kindly remember that.'

As Tiger slunk away to hide behind Flora's feet, Miss Watkyns looked at the children.

'I have something for you both,' she told them. 'From the Snergs.'

She pushed something across the desk.

'*Oh!*' said Pip. 'That's . . .'

'The Queen's Biscuit.' Flora said it for him.

Miss Watkyns nodded. 'You have an invitation. Perhaps Pip would like to read it.'

Getting to his feet, Pip took the biscuit. It felt light and crisp between his fingers, the message on it beautifully curled in royal icing. Very carefully, so as not to snap it, he laid it on the floor before turning his back and ducking his head between his legs. The orphans of Sunny Bay had been quick to adopt Gorbo's way with difficult words. Faced with a roomful of upside-down children, Mr Gribblestone had given up trying to stop it.

'It's exercise, of a sort.' He had justified this lapse of discipline to Miss Scadging. 'And a flow of blood to the head is known to be beneficial to the brain.'

Pip could hear the blood rushing past his ears as he

frowned at the iced words. His name and Flora's were easy to pick out – and that word, he knew, was *Queen*. Some of the rest he could guess.

'Her Majesty Queen Mercy of the Snergs . . .'

He didn't get any further. Tiger's memory for a telling-off was short. Nose twitching, he wriggled out from behind Flora's feet and pounced. In a matter of seconds, there was nothing left of the royal invitation but a few crumbs.

'Oh, *Tiger!*' said Pip and Flora together, in shocked reproach.

'Eating between meals,' said Miss Watkyns, 'is—'

'Against the rules?' suggested Flora.

'Discouraged,' said Miss Watkyns. 'I dare say he will sick it all up again.'

'Even if he does, we won't be able to *read* it,' said Pip sorrowfully.

'All is not lost,' Miss Watkyns told him. 'I know what it said. You two are invited to the Queen's feast. Gorbo is to be awarded the Brazen Nutmeg for bravery, however misguided, and loyalty to his friends. King Kul has dubbed him Honorary Knight Erratic, Sir Gorbo the Gormandizer

– they tried giving him his weight in string, but there was not enough to be found.'

'When do we leave?' Pip wanted to know.

'Now,' said Miss Watkyns, as a horn sounded. 'The Queen has made arrangements for your journey.

Sliding off the bench, the children scrambled to see out of the window. Out in the golden sunlight of the garden, the game of cricket was forgotten. A crowd of children watched with open mouths as an ostrich stepped neatly between the rowan trees. Perched on its back, Pompo blew another blast on his horn. Behind him ambled one, two, three cinnamon bears. Bouncing on the back of one of them – and grinning from ear to ear – was Gorbo.

'Gorbo!' The children rushed to the door. Flora reached it first; stopping suddenly, she turned and looked back at Miss Watkyns.

'I have something . . . there's something I've been meaning to give you,' she said. Reaching into her pocket, she held out her hand. From her fingers dangled a string of coral beads and half a little silver heart. 'She . . . someone gave it to me. But I think you ought to have it.'

'Thank you, Flora.' Miss Watkyns's expression was hard to read as she took the necklace. Unlocking the cabinet, she took out the ancient, barnacled tin box – in which two babies had once washed up on a beach. Lifting the lid, she picked something out. 'They have been separated,' she said, 'for a very long time.' Lying on her palm were both halves of a heart – one bright and shiny, the other tarnished and green.

'Nobody,' said Miss Watkyns, 'is born to be all good, or all bad. There is more than one side to every heart. What matters is, which side do you allow to rule you?' Shutting the box away again, she smiled at the children. 'Don't keep your friends waiting. It's time to go.'

'We're coming back though,' said Pip, in sudden alarm. 'Aren't we?'

'Other places are interesting,' agreed Flora, 'but here's where we belong – at Sunny Bay.'

'The day will come,' Miss Watkyns warned them, 'when the orphanage becomes too small for you. Like Heinrich Cornelius, you will need deeper waters to swim in.'

'Not yet, though,' said Pip. 'Not for ages.'

'Not yet,' agreed Miss Watkyns. Startling them very much, she bent to enfold them both in a quick hug. 'Go,' she ordered. 'Ride bears, dance on tables, eat cake by moonlight. And then come home.'

ACKNOWLEDGEMENTS

I am wary of elongated acknowledgements – who reads them, except for the one person you forgot to thank? – but I would never have strayed into the land of Snergs were it not for certain people.

This book owes its existence to Mr Wyke-Smith who first breathed life into Gorbo and Golithos, Mother Meldrum and Miss Watkyns. I hope very much that he would forgive me for the liberties I have taken – and for what I did to Baldry.

Heartfelt gratitude to Barry Cunningham and Rachel Leyshon at Chicken House for introducing me to the Snergs and offering me the opportunity to write this – it has been a privilege. Thanks to all the Chicken House team, especially to Rachel L and Laura Myers for untangling my knots and to Elinor Bagenal for working so hard to send Gorbo, Pip and Flora out into a world that had shut down.

I'm indebted to the Society of Authors, for a helping hand in a time of difficulty, also to the members, past and present, of the SCWBI Southampton group for their friendship and support. Particular thanks to my patient agent, Jenny Savill, also to Pauline and Tim Prentki for letting me write in the peace and quiet of their lovely house while my tortoise rampaged through their flower beds.

I cannot leave out Jeremy, inventor of robots and detector of bats, who has rescued me from a number of wobsers over the years and who unwittingly gave the Snergs their fondness for string.

Lastly, to the Snergs themselves: thank you – it's been marvellous.

THE EXTINCTS

George loves to help out at hidden Wormestall Farm, even though it's full of *extinctly* scary creatures, like the dodo in the dog bed and the dinosaurs in the duck pond. When Mortifer the giant basilisk goes missing, it's up to George to find him before wicked taxidermist Diamond Pye can add him to her stuffed animal collection . . .

This is a fabulously imaginative story and the characters are all great, particularly the wicked, vain and greedy Pye.
THE BOOKSELLER

Paperback, ISBN 978-1-911490-31-9, £6.99 • ebook, ISBN 978-1-911490-32-6, £6.99